Other books by

MICHAEL R. GOODWIN

SMOLDER
THE LIBERTY KEY

Short Story Collections

HOW GOOD IT FEELS TO BURN
ROADSIDE FORGOTTEN

Story Singles

THE RITUAL
CRIMSON GROVE
SPARROWS
KINDNESS
BROKEN JUSTICE

PRICE MANOR:

THE HOUSE THAT REMAINS

A NOVELLA BY

MICHAEL R. GOODWIN

The House That Remains: Book Three in the Price Manor series from Deadline Horror Collective. A horror novella.

For Jessica,

You are my safe haven, in which I will forever seek refuge.

"Don't fret precious, I'm here. Step away from the window; go back to sleep. Safe from pain and truth and choice and other poison devils. See, they don't give a fuck about you, like I do.

Counting bodies like sheep to the rhythm of the war drums."

-   A Perfect Circle

"Fortune, fame / Mirror, vain / Gone insane, but the memory remains."

-   Metallica

PRICE MANOR

The house appeared from behind a heat mirage, shimmering through the hot air rising off the hayfield that surrounded it. Only the second and third floors of the building were visible above the amber waves, making the structure look squatted and short. Upon closer inspection, it would become clear the house was anything but.

To say that the house was large would be an understatement. It was a massive feat of Gothic architecture, its many narrow windows staring back like a dead spider's eyes, its turrets and spires adorning the roof resembling a savage crown. An elaborate stone archway heralded the main entrance, and a stout iron fence traced around the perimeter.

For centuries, the field in which the house now sat had been home to nothing else except for whatever wildlife that passed through it. It was a place immune to time, one of the truly wild and untamed regions of Maine that man had yet to set foot on.

When the house appeared, snapping into existence with a concussive thump in the wide expanse of field, there was no one to witness it. The violent displacement of air and space sent a shockwave across the field in all directions, pressing the surrounding tall grass flat for nearly a hundred yards. The blast was so forceful that it tore a fox, which had been quietly stalking a mouse, to pieces.

The field mouse escaped without harm but the fox perished instantly, and the sound of the shockwave disturbed all of the birds in the trees for miles around.

Something else carried on the soundwaves, something more than just a rush of compressed air. The sound of a raging wildfire /of muskets blasting / of carnival calliope / of blood-chilling screams, all together at once carried across the field, each sound distinct and at the same time undistinguishable from the thunderclap it rode on.

It was this sound, and that of the birds taking flight, that alerted a small group of people traveling on foot a half-mile away that something had happened. All six of them turned toward where the sound had come from, eyes wide and apprehensive.

They huddled together, talking amongst themselves, while the house remained still and resolute in the field, waiting.

One of them pointed at the house, shimmering in the rising heat.

The house that had not been, but now was.

The house that was not just a house, but something more.

In the masonry of the stone archway, two words had been carved into the granite and inlaid with black marble, in an elegant but foreboding script.

PRICE MANOR.

In the field, the house remained.

WESLEY

Wesley had first watch.

He sat with his back in the corner, a pistol in one hand and a flashlight in the other, and surveyed the room. Moonlight filtered in through the curtains that had been made sheer with age, giving the ranks of bookcases that lined the opposing wall an eerie glow.

The library was dotted with overstuffed couches and chairs, providing a rare but appreciated luxury to the people that Wesley was traveling with. Normally they had only the ground to sleep on, so the opportunity to sleep on a cushion, even if it was dusty and smelled of mold and mice, was one none of them passed on.

There were five human-shaped lumps scattered across the library. Wesley rounded out the sextet, and having drawn the short straw, had the duty of keeping watch for the first half of the night. Dividing the night into shifts was nothing new for the group. They didn't take risks, and that was the only reason they had made it this far. He roved his eyes across the room: he checked the main door that led into the library from the foyer, the windows next, counted the slumbering bodies of his friends, and then made sure that the door to his left that led on to other rooms was still closed tight.

Right door clear, check the windows, count the bodies, left door closed, done.

There was something about this house that made him feel on edge, and as soon as they spotted the house a chill had run up his spine. It stood out in the field like a stain, a black tumor on the stunning landscape. But it was shelter when they had none, and the group did what they always did: they put it to a vote, and those in favor of seeking refuge in the house outweighed those who wanted to keep going.

Right door clear, check the windows, count the bodies, left door closed, done.

It made sense to hide out in the house. It looked like it was in shambles from the outside, uninhabitable, like a stiff breeze would knock it over. The disrepair was mostly on the exterior, they found, and aside from a thick layer of dust and an odd, stagnant smell, the inside was like a time capsule.

Right door clear, check the windows, count the bodies, left door closed, done.

The pistol felt foreign in his hand. He hadn't much experience with guns before society collapsed, but life in the apocalypse makes those who want to survive a quick study. He was a decent shot, but still hadn't grown accustomed to it. Sweat made his palms slick, but he kept his grip as tight as he could without causing it to cramp.

Forcing himself to take a deep breath, to try to stave off the nervousness and compulsory behavior that had controlled his entire life thus far, Wesley tried to do something that was very hard for him to do: relax.

As far back as he could remember, Wesley was in some sort of counseling or therapy. As a child, it was speech therapy. When that was fixed and he had it under control, his parents put him in anger management counseling, to help him learn to cope with pent-up anger from years of being bullied for having a stutter. Then, after a brief stint with no counselor or therapist at all when he first went to college, he realized he was so dependent on someone telling him how to act, how to behave, how to regulate his emotions, that he had a complete nervous breakdown.

Wesley was in the grocery store when it happened. It had been a bad day anyway, and having to shop in a crowded store certainly didn't help. A storm was coming in, and people were hoarding everything. The shelves were empty, and so soon became Wesley's reserve of patience.

All it took was someone snatching the last loaf of bread. When everything was said and done, he had stabbed five people: the loaf thief, and the four shoppers who tried to stop him from killing the guy.

He was charged and convicted and sent to where they sent all of the truly dangerous and insane in central Maine: Spring Meadow Psychiatric and Long-Term Care in Hamilton.

That was where he was when the apocalypse happened. Once everything really fell apart and the staff started caring more about themselves and their families than the incarcerated, Wesley knew he had to find a way to get out or risk being trapped inside.

On his way out the front door, dressed in another man's clothes and wearing another man's shoes, Wesley had the presence of mind to double back for a couple bottles of the anti-psychotics from the pharmacy. If he was going to blend in with the outside world, he needed to tame the urges that stabbing those people in the grocery store had unleashed.

Clive Wesley was a diagnosed psychopath with rage tendencies. What's worse, he was clinically trained through all of his years in therapy how to regulate himself, to blend in.

It was why he was able to fool this group of people he had been travelling with.

They didn't need to know about his past, or that Wesley wasn't even his first name.

They didn't need to know that he had killed six other patients and two devoted orderlies in order to escape Spring Meadow.

They especially didn't need to know that he was a few days away from running out of his anti-psychotic medication. If any of them had picked up on the fact that he seemed more nervous than normal, no one said anything. It was a byproduct of a reduced dose, having switched to half a pill to help stretch out whatever he had left.

Wesley could feel himself at war with the part of him he kept suppressed, but now wasn't the time to think about that. He needed to focus, to keep doing his job.

Blend in.

Right door clear, check the windows, count the bodies, left door closed, done.

He thought back to what Bruce, the oldest member of the group, said when they were voting about whether to go into the house. He protested heavily against it, insisting that the field the house sat in had always been just that… a field.

"Houses don't just appear," April countered. She was the lone female of the group, and often took charge of situations. Wesley had a notion that she was used to getting her way.

"I know that, but I'm telling you: *this* one did," Bruce had said. "This is Webster's Mills. I was born here, I grew up here, and aside from my time abroad in the Army, I've spent every day of my life here. I know every road, every farm, every field there is to know, and I'm telling you: that house was never there. It just showed up, somehow."

"No offense, but isn't it possible that you just… forgot that this one was here?" asked Tim. "You are getting on in years. Happens to the best of us."

Bruce had given Tim an icy glare at that remark. "Need I remind you that I was the Postmaster of this town longer than you've been alive? Advanced age or not, I think that I can be a trusted authority on this matter."

Wesley had then pointed out to the group that there was no mailbox on the street, and no driveway or road leading up to the house, both facts easily confirmed and supported Bruce's stance.

"Don't you think we owe it to ourselves to at least go check it out? No one is saying we have to move in, let's just investigate, see what we think, and regroup from there," John suggested. Both his name and physical appearance made him a dead ringer for John Coffey from *The Green Mile*, which was fitting as he was a major Stephen King fanboy.

"John has a point," Tim agreed. "Besides, the way I see it, even though it looks like a murder house, our choices are limited. We either go check it out, or we are left to decide between the swamp to our left, or the woods that M. Night Shyamalan made a movie about on the right."

A quick vote was held, and then the group made their way through the field toward the house. They moved as quickly as they could, for it wasn't safe to be out in the open for long.

Not when the Renegades were nearby.

Wesley blinked, bringing himself back to the present.

Right door clear, check the windows, count the bodies, left door closed, done.

They had been running from the Renegades for days now. As soon as they heard the diseased pulse of their war drums, they packed up their small campsite in Woolwich off the Kennebec River and traveled as quickly and as carefully as they could away from the sound. They managed only a few miles a day traveling on foot, as much as Bruce could manage.

Staying ahead of the Renegades was the only way they could ensure their survival. In the wastelands that was central Maine, the Renegades reigned supreme. A particularly nasty group of people, they were known to pillage and kill, taking whatever they wanted without morals or remorse or consequence. Rumors of cannibalism and ritualistic human sacrifice ran rampant, but one truth was evident: They use violence as a method of control, forcing submission and allegiance under the threat of horrible torture, mutilation, or death.

They travel endlessly, broadcasting the sound of war drums on loudspeakers to herald their approach. They enjoyed the hunt, and in the lawless world they now lived in, there was no one to stop them.

Wesley understood the appeal of the house, as it was so run down, so much in shambles that no one should dare go inside. Knowing the pattern of the Renegades, they would pass by without so much of a glance at it.

But as they got closer to the house, Wesley could see the confidence in those who voted in favor of checking things out begin to wane.

"That's some house," Brady, the youngest of the group, had observed as they approached.

"That's not a house; that's a mansion," April countered.

"It's not a mansion, either," Wesley had then said, pointing at the stone inlay in the archway that led on to the front door of the house. "It says PRICE MANOR."

The rest of the group looked up and saw, in the masonry of the stone archway that stood at the start of a narrow walkway, two words had been carved into the granite and inlaid with black marble, in an elegant but foreboding script.

"So it's not a murder house, after all," Tim said. "It's a murder *manor*. I have to admit, it's got a nice ring to it."

"Anyone else think it looks like the Marston House? You know, from *'Salem's Lot*?" John asked.

April groaned. "Always with the Stephen King references."

"I don't know about you guys," Tim said, ushering them all through under the archway toward the house, "but I'd rather face vampires than cannibals. Let's go."

Once inside, they did not venture far. The sun was setting, and they used their flashlights as sparingly as possible as batteries were a premium resource. John found the library and suggested that they setup camp in there for the night. He didn't have to lobby hard for that one, as once everyone saw the couches and sofas and chaise lounges, gone were most of the worries of the Renegades. They agreed they would explore the house tomorrow.

Wesley carefully set down the pistol, rubbed his hand on his jeans to wipe off the sweat, and checked his watch. It had only been an hour, and he doubted his ability to endure the remaining three. He was used to these night shifts, was used to watching over the people he had come to think of as friends, but there was something not right about this house.

When he first sat down in the corner for his shift, he tried to convince himself that it was just nerves. After that first hour, he stopped because the feeling of unease grew to the point where he could no longer ignore it.

He grabbed the pistol, his hand shaking, and swallowed hard.

He had to focus.

Wesley flicked his eyes to the right side of the room.

Right door clear, check the windows, count the bodies, left door...

The left door was open.

Wesley sat up straight, scared and surprised. He hadn't heard it open. He looked back over to the blanketed lumps of his group and counted.

April on the chaise lounge, John on the couch, Bruce on the overstuffed wingback, Tim on the couch opposite April, Brady on the...

Brady's couch was empty, his sleeping bag also missing. Brady himself was nowhere to be seen.

Where had he gone?

His mind began to race, immediately going to the worst-case scenario: that the group would think he had something to do with it. Even though Wesley was reasonably sure that none of them knew who he really was, the potential of getting caught was a very real fear. And in this case, he was innocent, but there was still some guilt on his responsibility. He was supposed to be on watch, of course.

Wesley slowly got to his feet. How had he missed Brady getting up and leaving the room? He knew he had gotten lost in thought a few times, but he was confident he would have noticed any one of them getting up and leaving.

He walked over to the door and looked through it. It led onto another room that was so dark that it was impossible to see beyond the doorway.

"Brady!" Wesley hissed, trying to keep quiet so to not wake the others. There was no response, so Wesley switched on his flashlight. The beam cut a swath of light into the gloom, revealing an empty room. He passed the flashlight over the walls, noting that there were no other doors or windows.

"Something wrong, Wesley?"

He turned and saw April sitting up, rubbing sleep from her eyes.

"Brady," was all he could manage to say.

"What about him?"

Wesley looked at the empty room, and then back to April.

"He's gone."

BRADY

Despite the comfort of the couch he laid on, Brady found himself unable to sleep. He wouldn't have thought it was possible, but he had grown accustomed to sleeping on the ground. Everyone else in the group didn't seem to share in his plight. Normally the sound of their snoring blended peacefully in with the other sounds of nature that surrounded them. Tonight, however, their snores were a source of frustration, taunting him with each passing minute.

He was used to being alone. His father left when he was two months old, and his mother died from a heroin overdose when he was fourteen. With no siblings, that left Brady to sort things out for himself. He buried his mother in the backyard behind their trailer and because he never reported his mother's death, her disability checks kept auto-depositing. Brady managed to fly under the radar until he graduated high school, and then the end of the world happened.

When the break-ins and looting in the trailer park started getting too close to home, Brady packed what he could carry in a backpack and left.

He spent only a few nights alone on the road before he realized he wouldn't survive long in the new lawless world by himself. He was too young, too inexperienced, didn't know enough about how the world worked to know how to handle himself. Brady's mother wasn't present much, and he never knew his father. All he knew was what he taught himself, and most of that had come from the internet.

Even though Brady had grown accustomed to solitude, he learned firsthand that there was strength in numbers. When he came across a quartet of travelers who offered to have him join with them, he readily accepted.

The security and comradery was nice, and he was good at following directions. But there were times where all Brady wanted was to be alone. This sleepless night was one of those times, and after an hour of lying awake, he couldn't take it anymore.

He could see Wesley sitting in the corner, fulfilling his duty as watchman for the first half of the night. Tim was supposed to take over in a few hours. Wesley took his responsibility as watchman seriously, his methodical and repeated scanning of the room gave Brady an opportunity to find some solitude, if he timed it right.

Brady had noticed that there were times when Wesley retreated in his mind. His eyes would go blank, glassy, and he wouldn't seem to be aware of anything going on around him. Wesley only did this when he thought no one else was watching, so all Brady had to do was wait for it to happen.

When at last it did, as Wesley was looking toward the right side of the room, Brady took action.

He slipped off the couch and, taking his sleeping bag with him, snuck across the room and prayed that the door on the far side of the library wasn't locked. Not only was it not locked, it opened easily and silently, as if the hinges had been recently oiled. That seemed odd, especially for a house that looked like it was a couple hundred years old, but Brady was too tired to question it.

The room was dark, and when he swung the door closed, Brady smiled. He couldn't hear the sound of snoring from the library, and he hadn't slept in complete silence and completely alone in so long. He would have felt giddy with excitement if he wasn't so exhausted.

In the dark, Brady spread out his sleeping bag and crawled inside. He slid his arm under his head as a pillow and felt himself slowly drifting off to sleep.

When he heard the whispering start, he thought he was dreaming.

It sounded at first like the way the tall grass sounded as it brushed against his legs, trudging through the field with the others to investigate the house that became known as Price Manor. The soft swishing sound swelled and grew until it became a voice, calling his name.

A female voice.

Brady, she called.

He stirred in his sleeping bag, caught on the fulcrum of consciousness and sleep, the corners of his mouth turning down.

Braaa-dy.

Another sound was introduced, and with it the feeling of someone running their hand up the length of his sleeping bag, searching for the zipper. Brady realized then that he wasn't sleeping, and he was too terrified to move.

There was someone in the room with him. They were calling his name, and they were trying to get into his sleeping bag.

"Brady," the voice said.

"April?" he asked, but there was no response.

He had feelings for April from the day she joined the group. She was older than him by close to a decade, but the strength she demonstrated while also appearing so fragile made his heart swell. Brady had never dated anyone, being the loner that he was all through high school, so he didn't know how to approach a girl his own age, much less a woman like April. He tried being chivalrous, tried finding reasons to be close to her, but he wasn't sure if he was broadcasting his intentions. Brady thought it might be easy to tell, but the way she acted toward him was hard to decipher. Women were hard to figure out.

A hand slid up his leg over the sleeping bag. Brady thought he caught a whiff of April's deodorant and excitement caught his breath. Had she been waiting for an opportunity for them to be alone, and followed him in here? The way she snuck in without him seeing was impressive.

The hand continued to slide up towards the top of the sleeping bag, and then it found the zipper. The zipper slowly pulled down, stopping halfway.

"April, I thought—"

He was interrupted by a set of lips pressing against his cheek, close to his lips. Brady was so caught off guard, so excited that this was finally happening, that it took him several moments to realize that something was wrong.

The lips were cold and dry, rough against his skin. He opened his mouth to speak and felt something tumble inside. It was lumpy and slimy and wriggling, and it crumbled into pieces as he worked it around his mouth.

It was dirt, rich and moist, and full of worms.

Brady gagged and pushed away, spitting out the mouthful of earth. He tried to get out of his sleeping bag, but whomever was in the room with him held the zipper tightly closed.

"I've missed you, Brady. Why did you leave me behind?"

He finally recognized the voice, and it was one he hadn't heard in several years. It made him freeze, a layer of dirt still clinging to the inside of his mouth.

The voice belonged to his mother.

He felt her hands brush hair out of his face, something she often did when she was still alive. Her hands were rough, grit caught in the grooves of her fingerprints. The coarseness of her skin scraping against his made him want to scream, but he found himself paralyzed.

"I was *so* lonely. Why don't you come back under with me?" Mother asked.

The smell of dry dust that pervaded the room faded, replaced with the cloying scent of freshly turned earth. The hardwood floor underneath his sleeping bag softened and Brady looked up to see the night sky. The stars got smaller and smaller as he sunk further down into the ground.

"Isn't this nice?" she asked. She had asked him the same question when they moved into the run-down trailer, the same one she eventually OD'd in. "It's cozy, isn't it?"

His mother's corpse wrapped her arms around him in a tight embrace. Brady tried to push away but she was too strong. He tried to yell for help but the dirt in his mouth had become like clay. His mother kissed him again, forcing more dirt and insects into his mouth.

Brady was trapped in every conceivable way.

But how was any of this happening? Was this an incredibly lucid dream?

18

Dirt began to tumble down on top of them. The sensation of it falling onto his face, the sound of it spattering down over his sleeping bag certainly didn't feel like a dream. It felt all too real, one of his worst fears realized: being buried alive.

The weight of the dirt pressing against him became suffocating very quickly. Soon he had dirt covering his entire face, trickling up his nose and into his ears. Brady began to thrash as the oxygen in his lungs ran out.

"*Shh*, Brady-my-baby," his mother said, using the pet name she had for him that he always hated. "I wasn't quite dead when you buried me. I woke up under there, scared and alone, wondering why Brady-my-baby would have left me like that. After some time I realized it wasn't so bad. Just relax. You'll see, soon you won't need to breathe."

His mother put her lips against his ear.

"You won't need to breathe because you'll be dead like me."

Brady could no longer hear the sound of dirt piling up on top of them. He assumed that meant they were too far underneath the surface to hear it. His body shuddered as he gave up on trying to breathe, gave up on trying to wake up from a nightmare that was, inexplicably, real life. He felt the cold earth pressing against him from all directions, felt the arms of his dead mother squeezing him tight, and then felt absolutely nothing.

Above him, the boards that made up the hardwood floor that had parted to bury him underneath the house slowly stitched back together, leaving no evidence at Brady had ever been there at all.

APRIL

"What do you mean, gone?"

Wesley's mouth opened and closed, as if he was trying to remember how to speak.

"I was sitting over there on watch," he said, gesturing with the pistol over to the corner, and by doing so sweeping it across the entire room, "and I don't know what happened. I noticed Brady wasn't on his couch, and that the door was open. I got up to investigate, and then you woke up."

"Okay, first thing's first, let me take that from you before you accidentally shoot someone," April said. She carefully took the pistol out of Wesley's hand, removing the magazine and locking the slide back. *Just in time, too,* she thought, noticing how badly his hands were trembling. She set the pistol down on a nearby bookshelf. "Take a deep breath, Wes. I'm sure he just went to find a place to go take a leak."

Wesley's flashlight was still pointed into the empty room. A thick layer of dust on the floor would have shown footprints, and the room was completely undisturbed. It smelled of freshly dug earth, a fact that April absently noted.

She operated best under pressure, and was often the first to step up and take action when others froze. This trait made her an asset when civilization ended, but it was exhausting. April confirmed she had her own pistol, secure in a holster on her waistband, and then gave Wesley's shoulder a light squeeze.

"Are you sure he went this way, in here?" she asked.

"No, I didn't see Brady at all. I guess I just assumed, because the door was open."

"So he could have gone out into the foyer, or literally anywhere else in this gigantic house?"

A groan from across the room made both of them turn.

"How many times do I have you remind you?" Tim said, his voice muffled from underneath his blanket. "This isn't a house. It's a *manor*."

"This isn't a time for jokes, Tim," Wesley said. "We have a problem. Brady is missing."

Tim sat up, tossing his blanket to the side. "The real problem is that you two don't know how to whisper, which is why I'm awake and talking to you instead of sleeping right now."

April sighed.

"Go back to sleep, Tim, unless you're going to help us look for Brady."

"I'm sure the kid can fend for himself. Besides, he like's being alone. He probably couldn't take anymore of Bruce's snoring. I've been thinking about stealing an empty bedroom myself."

April thought Tim was right. Brady was known for going off on his own. It fit a pattern of behavior that she had observed from him.

She made a point to watch everyone she was traveling with very closely, because April was not a very trusting person by nature. She trusted the men in her group enough, but this trait made life in the apocalypse very difficult. You had to constantly make decisions as to whether or not someone you encountered was someone who was going to help you or hurt you. That was why she carried a gun, because sometimes those situations changed quickly and without warning. It was why she was grateful she was born with the instinct to act quickly, and before the world fell apart that she had taken time to go through defensive firearm training. When April enrolled in the class, she hoped she would never have to pull the trigger in real life. Then, the definition of "real life" changed drastically.

She had pulled the trigger twice so far, both before joining forces with this group. Her aim was true both times, and she was still alive. She couldn't say the same for her adversaries.

"Okay, here's what we're going to do," April said, her voice taking on the authoritative edge that always commanded attention. "Wes, you're going to keep an eye on everyone here. I'm going to take your flashlight and go look for Brady. I'm sure he just needed some space, like Tim said, or maybe he needed to find a bathroom."

"I'm not sure it's a wise idea to be wandering off by yourself," Wesley said. "This house gives me the creeps."

April sighed. "There's not much to be afraid of when you've got a gun in your hand. I'll be fine."

"I agree with Wesley," came John's booming baritone in the dark. He clicked on a flashlight and propped himself up on one elbow. "Going somewhere alone in an abandoned house is a rookie mistake. Trust me, I've seen a lot of horror movies, and nothing ever good comes from it."

Bruce cleared his throat clicked on his flashlight, too. "We might as well divide up into groups and go look for him, because none of us will catch a wink of sleep with all this chit-chat."

Tim groaned and threw off his blanket. "Old man has a point. Let's get this over with."

April motioned for the group to gather in the center of the library, where Brady had been sleeping.

"Okay, Bruce and Tim, you take the first floor. John, you and I will go upstairs and see what we can find," April said, and everyone nodded in acceptance of their charge.

Wesley waited expectantly for his instructions, and when they didn't arrive, he balked.

"What about me?"

"You're on watch, so you stay here in case Brady comes back. If he does, give us a holler," April replied, and without giving Wesley a chance to refused, pushed through the group and made her way to exit the library into the foyer. "Come on, the sooner we find the kid, the sooner we can all go back to sleep."

They broke off into groups, leaving Wesley behind in the library. April felt a twinge of regret for leaving him by himself, but honestly, he really needed to just grow a pair. A couple minutes, maybe an hour by himself would do him some good. April had a suspicion that not much had been asked of him in his life before everything went to hell.

"Let's regroup in an hour if we haven't found him," April said when they were all out in the foyer. "I don't think it will take that long to find him. He couldn't have gone far."

Bruce and Tim nodded and went off into the west side of the house.

April looked to John, who gestured up the massive staircase that led to the upper floors.

"Ladies first," he said.

"Who said I was a lady?" April replied, and gestured for him to go ahead of her.

John smiled, as if he expected this response from her, and took the stairs. April pulled the pistol out from her holster and gripped it with both hands, right index finger along the trigger guard, muzzle pointed toward the floor.

The defensive handgun course taught her how to clear a house, how to hold the pistol to direct recoil into her shoulders and torso, how to bring the pistol into her sightline and level it at the threat, how to pull the trigger and keep in motion to place follow-up shots. It taught her that you don't take warning shots.

At first, going to the class seemed excessive to her friends, her family, but April paid them no attention. They didn't have the same concerns as her. They didn't have a stalker.

Dustin was a guy she met at work. He transferred into her department and seemed nice enough. Friendly, tall, and that killer smile certainly helped wear down her normal and strict "no office romances" policy. Two dates in and his demeanor changed, and he had a hard time being told 'no'.

April managed to get away from him, grateful that she made sure their dates all were in public places. As she ran from him, though, and for months following, she could still feel his hand sliding up her leg, and the way he dug his nails in when she tried to push his hand away.

He had plenty of excuses for being so forward, for not listening, but April knew where things would have gone if she hadn't pulled out the pepper spray from her purse.

24

The incessant phone calls and texts were annoying but tolerable, at all hours of the night. Then at work, he found excuses to be close to her, took his breaks at the same time, even went out of his way to park next to her in the parking garage. She reported his behavior to HR and he was immediately fired due to their 'no tolerance' policy.

His harassment of her went to another level after that. He began making threats in his voicemails and text messages, leading April to block him, but Dustin would just change his number. He started spreading vile rumors about her to his former colleagues, and though all of this April thought she was doing all she could.

All she had done was tell him she didn't want to sleep with him. She didn't deserve any of this fallout.

She made her first police report when he started following her to work, and then back home. He would sit outside in his car on the street, watching her house. Dustin followed her to a family barbeque for her father's birthday, bursting in through the front door and accusing her of cheating on him until he realized this was her childhood home.

It took for that to happen for her family to finally understand what April had been talking about for months.

A police report was filed, and soon after a judge granted a restraining order against him.

At that point, she realized pepper spray might not be enough someday.

April enrolled in the defensive firearm course, and two weeks later society collapsed. There was no police, no law enforcement of any kind. The restraining order was just a piece of paper now, and April wasn't sure what Dustin was going to do, now that there were no repercussions for him.

She didn't have to wait long, as he let himself into her apartment one night, just two weeks after the local police department disbanded and the worst of the looting was over. April had stockpiled food and supplies, a habit from growing up during the COVID years, so she hadn't needed to leave.

And she was waiting for him.

Dustin kicked down her door, and April emptied the pistol's magazine into his chest.

Her instructor's voice echoed in her head. *Don't stop shooting until you run out of ammunition, or until the threat is eliminated.*

In this case, it was both.

April reloaded her pistol with a fresh magazine as she stood over his dead body, making sure he was fully gone before doing anything else. Then, she grabbed her pack that she had ready, and left her apartment behind.

Living in fear of Dustin coming after her left April with some lasting trauma, something that she didn't quite dare to call PTSD even though it sure fit the definition. It made her hyper vigilant, always on guard, and always the first to be in charge.

It was why she was able to order around a group of men, some twice her age or more, as if they were schoolchildren.

April allowed herself a small smile as she continued up the stairs.

TIM

Forever known as the "Chandler" of any group of people, everyone found it hard to take Tim seriously. That is in part due to his incessant wisecracking, but it didn't take a psychotherapist to surmise that all the jokes and sarcasm was a cover for all the things about himself that Tim didn't want others to see.

Humor was his shield, his main defense against people getting too close, against people who abandoned him, against people realizing that underneath it all, he was horribly insecure.

Tim hid his insecurities exceedingly well, and truth be told, he didn't mind being known as the funny guy. There were worse things in life to be, and he had a repertoire of jokes for nearly every social situation that was unmatched.

Jokes didn't seem to matter as much in the dystopian aftermath, but some people still knew the value and restorative nature of laughter. Nearly everyone in the group was good mannered in that way, a true stroke of luck, but Bruce had been a tough egg to crack. Tim considered it a personal achievement the day he got the old man to smile.

"Where do you think the kid went?" Tim asked. He wanted to ease gently on the humor in this case, because he knew Bruce had formed an unlikely kinship with Brady. He was constantly offering the boy advice, like a father does to his son, and Brady soaked it up like a dry sponge.

"Darned if I know," Bruce grumbled, "but at my age, the only thing that gets me out of bed before sunrise is my bladder. Maybe he just needed to take a leak."

"Who knows where the bathroom is in this place. I feel like I'd need a map to not get lost."

Bruce sighed and moved toward what looked like a kitchen, and Tim followed close behind. He looked around as they went, marveling at the elaborate woodwork. Roses and other flowers had been carved into the wood.

The silence between them soon grew too awkward for Tim to bear, so he grasped for something to talk about.

"Still believe this house appeared out of nowhere?" he asked, and then winced. Open mouth, insert an old man's angry foot.

Bruce stopped in the entrance to the kitchen and turned around.

"Actually I do. And because you never seem to take anything seriously, I'm not going to tell you why," he said. "You'll just make a joke about it."

"I can be serious. Humor is just a defense mechanism," Tim said, which is a statement he had uttered many times over the years, but still no one thought he was being serious.

Bruce leveled his eyes at Tim, a sensation that was as uncomfortable as it was terrifying, and then grunted.

"Not worth the time or the breath to tell you," he decided, and then entered the kitchen.

"Come on, Bruce. I promise to not make a single joke out of whatever you say about this house from here on out," Tim pleaded, running ahead to get in front of

Bruce. Bruce stopped walking, and Tim offered his hand. "You have my word."

"Your word, eh?" Bruce speculated. "Well, if your word is as strong as your jokes are, then we might have a problem."

Tim was stunned at the insult, but then saw the corner of Bruce's lip turn up in a smile.

"I'm just messing with you," Bruce said, laughing. "Figured it was only fair, considering you mess with everybody else all the darned time."

Tim smiled as Bruce took his hand and gave it a firm shake. "I guess even an old dog has its tricks."

The laughter between them diminished, and Tim noticed an echo repeating it back to them. The existence of the echo wasn't what stood out, but rather the way the echo *sounded*. It wasn't a true echo, but more like someone (or some*thing*, Tim thought with a shudder) was trying to imitate the sound of their laughter. And not just Tim's or Bruce's separately. Both at once.

Tim looked at Bruce, who returned a startled expression.

"You hear it, too?"

Bruce only nodded.

The sound was eerie and haunting, and it was getting louder.

Closer.

The kitchen was barren. Blank spaces where appliances might have once been, cabinet doors hanging askew, a tangle of cobwebs draped over the deep sink.

On the tiled floor, crisscrossing and overlapping footprints made Tim jump.

Someone else had been through here.

The echo changed suddenly, the laughter becoming a shriek, like the sound of a woman screaming, as if she were in terrible pain. The increase in volume gave away its location, and both Tim and Bruce spun around to the far wall, where a tall wooden cabinet stood. A set a buttons on the wall indicated to Tim that it was likely a dumb waiter.

"What the hell is going on?" Tim said.

Bruce pushed Tim out of the way, brandishing a length of broom handle that had been laying on the ground. He gripped it like a baseball bat as he approached the dumb waiter.

It occurred to Tim then that it was odd no one else from the group had come to see what all the screaming was about. How could they not hear it?

He turned around toward the kitchen door and noticed that it was closed, the thick double doors pressed firmly together. Panic rose in his chest. He wasn't claustrophobic, but he certainly wasn't a fan of being closed up with whatever was making that noise.

It reminded him of something from his childhood, a memory he worked very hard to banish.

The house he grew up in had a small brook that wove its way down from a lake that was a few miles up the road. In the spring it was more like a river, as the lake could not contain all of the water runoff coming down from the mountains from melting snow and ice.

When the brook swelled into a river, all of the grass and brush grew in thick and tall, sometimes reaching the height of young Tim's waist. He would push his way through to the flat rock he would spend hours sitting on, watching the small fish that made the journey downstream.

There was an influx of wildlife that came hand in hand with the spring runoff. Plenty of birds and squirrels, but those were commonplace. If Tim sat still enough, a raccoon or a muskrat would make its way to the water's edge. He would spend hours out there, marveling at how connected everything in nature was.

As soon as the sun would start to go down, Tim would leave. Nature was beautiful and intriguing in the daylight, but dusk and dark changed everything.

At night, the nocturnal animals came out, and they came out at night for a reason. They were the predators, the animals that stalked and killed their prey under the cover of darkness. And there was one particular animal that frightened Tim the most.

The appearance of the Runoff River (as Tim's father called it every year) brought many different flora and fauna, but one year it brought a breed of bird that was exceedingly rare in North America, much less in the quiet rural area of Hamilton, Maine.

Tim was in bed reading one night when he heard a scream tear through the silence of the evening. He dropped his book and ran out into the living room, where his parents sat watching television.

It sounded like a woman screaming, and it was coming from across the street. From the river.

His parents weren't sure of what it was, but they also didn't want to venture outside to investigate.

"I'm sure it is just an animal," Tim's mother said, ushering him back to bed. "Here, let me turn the radio on, maybe that will help cover the sound."

She turned on the radio, the soft rock of Steve Miller's "Fly Like an Eagle" doing very little to hide the sound of the bird calling, but it did help. Eventually he fell asleep, but it was plagued with nightmares.

The next day, Tim spotted an owl roosting in a hollow of a dead tree. He noted its distinct appearance, and after begging his mother to take him to the library, he found a book about owls of the world. He flipped through it until he spotted a glossy photo of the same owl he saw in that hollow.

It was a barking owl, which Tim found odd. This owl didn't bark. It *screamed*, sounding exactly like a woman in terrible pain.

And it screamed every night for an hour for the next three nights.

Each night it would send him running to the living room, to the embrace of his mother who did her best to calm him down. On the third night, as she was putting Tim back to bed, she sat on the edge of his bed and asked him what made it so scary, especially after knowing what was making the sound.

"It's the bad dream," he confessed.

"You've been having nightmares?" she asked. "Want to tell me about them? Maybe it won't seem so scary if you talk about it."

Tim didn't want to say it out loud, for fear it would come true. He just cried, and eventually he fell asleep, opening up the gateway for the dream to happen yet again.

The dream began like it always did: it was nighttime, and the owl was screaming. In the dream he was feeling brave, and wanted to confront the bird and scare it away. With a flashlight in one hand and a cap gun in the other, he snuck out of the house. He turned back once to look through the living room windows, and thought it odd that his parents weren't sitting in their usual spots, watching TV. He shrugged it off and walked down the front lawn, across the street, and then down into the thick brush toward the gurgling river.

A wide path had been made in the brush, the grass pushed aside and matted down. The owl screamed, and there was the sound of thrashing further down toward the water. Tim was scared, but he had come this far. He wasn't going to turn back now.

It was only a few more paces to reach the water's edge, and when Tim's flashlight cut through the grass and illuminated the water, there was no preparing himself for what he saw.

His father was kneeling in the river, holding someone down under the water. His shirt was bloody and torn, and he was soaking wet. Cords of muscle stood out on his forearms, straining to keep the person down, who was thrashing violently.

The flashlight distracted his father from his task and he looked up, surprised. A momentary lapse in focus allowed his victim a chance to push up and out of the water.

It was a woman, and Tim would have recognized her anywhere.

It was his mother, and she screamed.

It sounded just like the scream of the owl.

"Go back to bed, Tim," his father said through gritted teeth, pushing his mother back down under the water. "It's just an owl, remember?"

Tim's father then changed up his grip, holding Mother down under water by her neck with his left hand, freeing up his right to select a large rock from the riverbank.

The flashlight slipped from Tim's trembling hands, landing so that the light cut an angled swath across both the water where his mother lay trapped and the upper half of his father.

The owl screamed, and Tim's father brought the rock down on his mother's head. The water became red, and the owl screamed.

The world was reduced to the noises that enveloped him. The sound of the rock crashing repeatedly in the water, the incessant babble of the river that carried his mother's blood and bone and brain matter downstream, and the sound of the owl screaming.

When Tim woke the next morning, he thought nothing of the dream, but it had been an exact replay of the dream he had ever since that owl showed up. He left his bedroom, glad for the sun, and went into the kitchen for breakfast.

But Mother and Father were nowhere to be seen. The coffee pot wasn't even on.

Tim looked to the front door and saw two pairs of boot prints, his father's and his own.

A trail of water shined on the linoleum, and Tim followed it to his parent's bedroom.

Tim's father lay on his bed, the top half of his skull obliterated by the shotgun barrel he had in what remained of his mouth. A viscous spray adorned the headboard and the surrounding walls, but the white envelope on the foot of the bed had been spared.

Tim, it read.

But Tim ran out of the room, pulled on his boots, and then ran down to the river across the street. Had his nightmare been real? Had he witnessed his mother being murdered by his father?

Tim arrived at the riverbank and saw his mother's body lying askew in the water, her skull bearing a disturbing resemblance to his father's. A fox was chewing on her hand, trying to make off with one of her fingers.

What happened next was a blur. There were hazy patches where he remembered going back inside and calling 9-1-1, and then it was a flurry of police officers and hospitals and social workers. Then, he was placed into a group home for a few months until the state was able to locate his only other living relative, his mother's sister. She stepped up and took him into her home.

He didn't know she existed until a social worker told him where he was going to live. Despite being unknown to each other, his aunt treated him as if he were her own child right from the start. They shared a bond, as both of them had endured horrible things in their lives, and they both carried scars from it. His were emotional, whereas hers were physical.

She told him that the day they met. She knew his story, but Tim never found out what had happened to her. She always told him she would when he was older, but when he reached adulthood and still she refused, he had a feeling that age had nothing to do with it.

She encouraged him to speak with a therapist about what he had gone through, and it was through these sessions that Tim uncovered repressed memories about the worst week of his life.

As it turned out, there had never been a barking owl.

The screams he heard were those of his mother, being beaten by his father. Testimony from his mother's friends and co-workers corroborated this.

And now, three decades after these horrible events, Tim had to remind himself that the screams he was hearing were not his mother, begging for her life.

Maybe this time it really was a barking owl. Or maybe it was something else entirely.

It would have been easier to believe if Tim didn't also hear the babbling of the Runoff River, which he knew was just an auditory hallucination, but that didn't stop the gooseflesh from rising on his skin.

Tim jumped when Bruce dropped a hand on his shoulder.

"You okay?" Bruce asked.

Tim shook his head to clear his thoughts. "Yeah, was just reminded of something."

"A bad something, by the looks of your face."

"You could say that, but it's not something I care to remember or talk about, so please don't ask," Tim said, coming off a little more strong than he intended.

Bruce shrugged. "Wasn't planning on it. In my generation, men didn't talk about their problems. We just drank."

"Wouldn't mind a drink right about now," Tim said. "Let me see that broom handle."

Tim took it from Bruce before it could be given to him, and then he strode up to the dumb waiter and beat the wooden handle against it as hard as he could.

After a few moments of thrashing the door, the screaming faded. All that was left was the sound of the water gurgling over the riverbed, and as Tim's blood pressure dropped to a normal level, he found that the sound of the river faded, as well.

"I suppose you're not going to tell me what that display of anger and savagery was all about, either," Bruce remarked.

"And circle gets the square."

At this, Bruce laughed, and Tim was shocked. He hadn't even made a joke this time.

"I didn't think you were old enough to have watched *Hollywood Squares*. It was Helen's favorite show," Bruce said, and at the mention of Helen's name the happiness on his face became stained with sadness.

"Helen. That was your wife?"

Bruce nodded. "For 47 years, yes. She's gone now."

Tim would normally say something funny at a moment like this, to help break up the tension and the heavy emotion, but knew this was hard for Bruce to talk about. He stayed quiet out of respect, to allow Bruce to take the lead of the conversation.

"We were down in Portland, at Maine Medical Center," Bruce continued. "She hadn't been feeling well for a few days, and when we walked in, her heart stopped. Docs got her back, but she never woke up. In the end, I reckon that was a blessing. She passed just a few days before the worst of things. I'm sure you've heard by now what happened there when things got really bad."

Tim nodded. The worst rioting Maine had ever seen took place in Portland. He only got to see the aftermath of it, which was to say that he saw what was left of it, once the bombing and the fires had done their worst.

"Once she died and the riots started gathering momentum, I took our car and just drove, got out of the city as fast as I could. Followed the coastline, because Helen loved the ocean more than anywhere else in the world. Ran out of gas, couldn't find a gas station that hadn't already been ransacked, so I just started walking."

"And then you ran into a smartass who wouldn't leave you alone," Tim said, allowing himself to smile.

Bruce smiled, too. "Worst decision I ever made, letting you tag along."

Tim laughed. "You didn't have much of a choice. You're too slow on foot."

The two men enjoyed the moment of mirth they shared, for there had been few of them since they met.

37

Life on the road was hard, and finding yourself as prey to human predators made it even worse.

"Think there's any booze in this place?" Bruce asked, having forgotten about looking for Brady.

Tim clapped Bruce on the shoulder. "Now we're talking. Let's have a look."

JOHN

The stairs were oddly quiet, for a house as old as this one seemed to be. John crept up them slowly at first, until he realized that he wasn't trying to sneak up on anyone. Then he took them several at a time and reached the first landing in just a few strides.

"Hold up, wait for the short kid," April said.

John looked around as he waited for April to catch up.

"This place sure is spooky," he said, his deep voice echoing up to the third floor.

"Big guy like you, getting scared by an abandoned house? I find that very surprising," April replied, reaching the landing. She had both hands gripped onto her pistol, and John thought she looked like a member of a SWAT team.

He stepped aside and let her take the lead down the hallway, holding his flashlight up to show the way.

"Where did you learn to use a gun like that? Were you in the military? Police?" he asked.

"Nope, just another woman who got fed up with being scared of the patriarchy."

The way she answered his question told John that there wasn't room for more questions, and he certainly didn't want to open the floor for debate when she was holding her pistol like a seasoned cop, so he decided to change the subject.

"Do you really think Brady went up here?" he asked.

"It doesn't look like anyone has been up here in decades," April replied. "You'd think we'd be able to see footprints in the dust if he did come through here, like the ones were making."

"Good point." John looked back the way they came, seeing April's small footprint dwarfed by his own. "So why are we even up here?"

"So we can have confidence the area is secure."

The precision in her tone told John more about April than anything else she had told him so far. This wasn't just a casual search of the house for her. This was a mission.

"Well, once we're done with securing the upstairs, do you think we should look outside?" John suggested. "Maybe he went out for some fresh air. Might save ourselves a bunch of time."

April paused.

"Why didn't I think of that? We should have looked there first."

From further down the hall, past where the flashlight could reach, a door slammed closed. Both John and April turned toward the noise, John aiming his flashlight down into the dark, April raising her pistol up into firing position.

"Maybe he is up here after all," John said.

"Must be," April agreed, but there was a shade of doubt in her voice. It could have been fear, and if it was, it would mark the first time John had noticed it.

April seemed incapable of fear, always taking the lead. John was grateful for that, as in his life before, many people had looked to him for that, and he was glad for the break.

John had always been big, in a thick, muscular way, never in an overweight, unhealthy way. As a child, his mother saw to that, making sure he ate well and played as many sports as he could manage. He was naturally athletically gifted, that much was clear. A wave of success and popularity from his athletic prowess started in junior high, and he rode that wave through high school and into adulthood. He loved the attention, loved pushing himself physically, and had grown accustomed to being the leader of any group he found himself in.

Despite many scholarship offers for him to play football or basketball for different schools, when John graduated high school, he became a firefighter. He felt that he should use his God-given abilities to do good for others. He rose quickly through the ranks, and was soon to be captain of his firehouse at Bramhall Station.

Things had been rough during the times of COVID, but that did little to prepare any of the first responders for the next wide-spreading virus that would eventually make society in America fall apart.

A lab-made variant of leprosy, cooked up as an experiment that somehow left the sterile protection of the facility it was made in, was what sent everything in a tailspin. Those who were exposed to an infected individual saw lesions spread quickly over their body, and they would become septic within 48 hours. Overwhelming pain from the festering boils and rotting open sores usually paved the way for high fevers, and if they didn't succumb from fever-induced seizures within the first week, the vast majority committed suicide to free themselves of the all-consuming pain.

It was chaos, to say the least, but absolute pandemonium broke out when it became known that there was no viable possibility for a cure or a vaccine to stop its spread. Due to the complexity of the virus and how it mutated each time it spread, any potential vaccine needed to be specifically modified for the individual person who was infected. Developing a single cure would take two weeks, 10 days at best.

By then, the patient would be dead.

John got to witness firsthand how the community of people he had spent his whole life with change. From close-knit to every-man-for-himself in a matter of one day, those who were afraid of catching the disease stayed indoors. Those who wanted to take advantage of an overwhelmed and exhausted police force by looting grocery stories, pharmacies, and hospitals took their anger to the streets.

There was no military backup to support them. There was no cavalry to call in. As the situation became increasingly dire, the men and women first responders of Portland took it to a vote: continue to protect and serve, or abandon post so that they could protect their own families.

The vote to disband was a landslide, and John, who had been working for 48-hours straight at the time of the vote, rushed home to his family.

He found his wife Amanda dead at the kitchen table, a bottle of pills clutched in her hand. Streaks of lesions, the distinct markings of this horrid virus, ran up her forearm. She had taken her life to avoid going through the horrible pain that was sure to come.

But where were their two children? They were only four- and five-years old. Surely she wouldn't have…

When John found them in the bathtub, floating face down, he fell to his knees. Lesions spotted their skin from head to toe, and he immediately understood what had happened.

He had heard about parents committing murder-suicide to escape the horrible death that would inevitably come, but never thought it would happen in his own home. John, who had always been peaceful and calm in the face of anger and calamity, broke down. This was an adversity far too great for him.

There was nothing left for him. No family, no job, and no community left to serve. Everything had gone to hell, and he was left behind to live it in. Unable to stay in his house, knowing what his wife had done in desperation to spare her children and herself from a horrible death, John left.

He walked away with no supplies, no gear, nothing. He didn't care if he survived, as everything he had to live for had been taken from him. He contemplated death, but in the end he was still a leader, even in the depths of his grief and despair. People still turned to him to help, even complete strangers on the street.

It was how he came to be with this group, and when April joined in and starting barking orders in tense situations, all John felt was relief. She was clearly more than capable, and he was glad to let her take charge.

But there was something about the energy in this house that made him feel like maybe this time, they should both be on the front line instead of him following behind her.

"April, hold up," John said. "Something doesn't feel right."

His voice came out in a whisper, and April didn't seem like she heard him. She crept down the hallway toward where it made a 90-degree turn to the right.

"Hold on, April, wait for me to catch up," he called out, and now found that his feet felt like they were stuck in mud. He aimed his flashlight down and saw that a set of hands had sprouted out from the moth-eaten rug.

They gripped hard around his ankles, hooking into the laces of his work boots. John tried to lunge out of their grasp, but only succeeded in pulling whomever was somehow hiding underneath the floorboards further out.

He looked back down the hallway toward April, hoping she would notice he was not behind her anymore, but she was gone. She must have turned the corner, but that didn't explain why she didn't hear him. The entire house had been silent.

The hands tried to pull him down into the floor. John felt a sense of vertigo as he sunk down, but he couldn't allow that to happen. Though he was still tall, the lack of daily workouts and strenuous labor that his job at the firehouse demanded rendered him weaker than he would have liked, and whatever had latched onto him was *strong*. Unnaturally so.

"Help me, April!" he cried.

John had always been an avid reader of horror books and watcher of horror movies, but this real-life horror terrified him. He never felt fear when staring down a burning building or having to perform a dangerous and tense rescue. There had always been this part of him that saw those moments as a challenge, one that could be defeated. He had great instincts, instincts that had been finely honed over his entire life, and all of them now had apparently disappeared.

John tried to run and immediately fell, landing flat on his face. The flashlight fell from his hand and spun across the floor. He felt the hands release his feet, so he rolled over and tried to push himself back and away.

"April!" he yelled, desperate, and this time he knew it was loud enough for her to hear. So why was she not coming back for him?

The creature from underneath the floor jumped out from under the rug, covered in dust and dirt and cobwebs. It moved in jerky, unsteady motions, yet somehow much faster than John. A cone of light cut diagonally across the hallway from where the flashlight had landed, and as the creature jumped on top of John, the fear within him having turned his muscles to jelly, he recognized who the creature was.

"Amanda?"

BRUCE

When Bruce laid his head back in his chair a few hours before, he was sure he would lie awake until sunrise. He didn't require much sleep these days, but on this night, his restlessness had nothing to do with how tired he felt, and everything to do with where he was.

There was something wrong with this house.

It shouldn't be here.

Until today, he was confident, it *hadn't* been here.

There was a small voice in his mind, however, that was siding with the doubtful members of his group. Maybe he had forgotten. Maybe it had always been here.

But no. He spent nearly five decades of his life in the postal service, and Webster's Mills was the poster child for the rural, small-town vibe in Maine. It's only claim to fame was its annual fair, which drew vendors from out of state and patrons from even further, giving the local businesses the boost in income that they very much needed in order to make it another year.

No, he was sure that he would have known this house, because his brain contained a map of Webster's Mills that was as detailed as any you'd find elsewhere. Bruce knew every road there was to know, especially a main drag as heavily travelled as Route 17.

The field this house sat in had always been vacant, as far back as he could remember. The property owner, Ed Bartlett, let it run wild, not even bothering to hay the field to make a little money on the side.

Bruce asked him about it once, when Ed came in to the post office to send out a parcel.

"You going to hay that field down on 17 this year? Hay is fetching a pretty penny, from what I've been hearing."

Ed shook his head. "I'll tell you what my father told me, and his father before him: that field is God's field. I've got plenty of other fields to hay and plant crops in. That one, she'll remain untouched. Have you seen the view from that field?"

Bruce had, of course, and it was an impressive view indeed. It was a vista unrestricted by power lines, unblemished by houses or buildings. All you could see to the horizon was the beauty of nature, sloping mountains, and the occasional blue pocket of water. He had admired this view countless times, and aside from the changing seasons, it never changed.

He remembered casting a side-eyed glance at that view on the way through to Gardiner, his wife Helen in the passenger seat, wrapped in an afghan she knitted herself. She hadn't been feeling well for a few days, and started getting a bad looking rash on her forearms. It didn't take much convincing to get her to the doctors, which was an indicator to Bruce as to just how sick she felt.

When he drove by, the field was just as Ed Bartlett intended. Empty.

Except now, there was a house, this ancient goliath that Bruce knew for sure, old age or not, had not existed prior to his trip down to Portland. And that was only a few weeks ago, a month at most.

But that wasn't the only reason this house had him feeling unsettled.

47

He knew more about this house than he was letting on.

Bruce grimaced as he took a sniff from the Mason jar Tim had found under the kitchen sink.

"I'm pretty sure this is paint remover," Tim said, screwing the lid back on the jar, "and just smelling it killed off as many brain cells as a night at the bar."

Tim bent over to put the jar back underneath the sink, and Bruce stuck out his foot to block the cabinet door from opening.

"Clearly you've never had the pleasure of Maine moonshine," Bruce said, taking the jar out of Tim's hands. He unscrewed the lid and took a pull. Liquid fire traced its way to his stomach, and he grunted when it landed. He then handed the jar to Tim. "Your turn."

Tim took it but looked suspiciously at the liquid inside. "What doesn't kill you makes you stronger, right?"

"This will sterilize you from the inside out," Bruce said with a laugh.

"Good. I've never wanted kids." Tim took a sip from the jar and coughed it down.

Bruce put the lid back on and waited for Tim to recover.

"As my father used to say, that'll put some hair on your chest," Bruce said.

He dusted off the counter and leaned against it.

"We going to keep looking for the kid?" Tim asked. He got up onto the counter next to Bruce.

"Yeah, in a minute. There's something I want to talk to you about, and even though you don't always seem to take things seriously, I have a feeling that's just a front. You're a level-headed guy, am I right?"

Tim nodded, seeming impressed with Bruce's insight.

"I thought so. Keep that mind open wide, as what I'm going to tell you is going to seem like I'm crazy. But I assure you, I'm not."

Tim nodded, his eyes already getting a little glassy from the moonshine.

Bruce sighed, as he wasn't much for talking, much less about himself, and what he had to say was a lot to take in.

"Ever since I was a kid, I remember hearing these stories. I guess you call them 'urban legends' now, but one of the stories that I found the most interesting was about a house that just... *appears*. One time it happened during a wildfire in Oregon. Another time in Russia in the mid-1800's. England in the 1600's. Various different locations, different times... But in each occurrence, this large house would just suddenly appear," Bruce said.

"Like you claim this house did, you mean?" Tim said, his voice slurring.

This guy cannot hold his liquor, Bruce thought.

"Right," Bruce said. "Where once there was no house, there suddenly was. And almost as quickly as it showed up, it would disappear as if it was never there. And nearly anyone who went inside never came back out."

Tim's eyes widened.

"So you mean... they die?" he asked.

"One can presume."

Tim swallowed hard and wiped a hand over his face.

"I think I'm going to need another drink from that jar," he said.

"You and me both," Bruce agreed.

Another drink was had, and Bruce gave time for Tim to think.

"Do you think that's what this place it? That this is the traveling house from some urban legend?" Tim asked after a few minutes had elapsed.

Bruce shrugged. "I don't know. It might be, but the more I think about it, the less I seem to remember. It almost feels like it doesn't want me to remember."

"That what doesn't want you to remember?" Tim asked.

Bruce caught Tim's eye. "Something within the house itself."

Tim said nothing for another moment, and then sighed.

"Let's say your suspicions are right, and that this house is what you claim it to be. By those rights, it's not likely we are going find Brady at all."

"Not alive, no. He probably died hours ago," Bruce replied.

Tim got down slowly from the counter. "And this house, whatever controls it, is going to actively try to kill us all?

"That's the long and short of it, yes. What do you think that screaming thing was, in the dumb waiter? It sure seemed to strike a nerve with you, and I have a good reason to believe you know exactly what it was."

Tim's eyes widened, and Bruce saw the truth settle into him.

"Why didn't you say anything, before we came in here?" Tim asked.

"I tried to tell you all that it was a bad idea, but I got out voted. You know that."

Bruce locked eyes with Tim, who looked more scared than Bruce had ever seen him.

"Well if you had told us about this shit, we might have been more willing to think things out," Tim said, exasperated. "And you came in here with us, knowing that you'd probably not make it out alive. Why would you do that?"

That was the question Bruce was still trying to find an answer for himself.

"If I'm being honest," he began, "it's because I've taken a shine to you all and if there was any way I could protect you, I'd be more able to do so from the inside than from the outside."

Tim feigned a shocked expression. "So the old man *does* have a heart!"

"Grinch-sized, but yes."

A heavy thud and the sound of something scurrying away came suddenly from the dumb waiter, and both Bruce and Tim turned toward it. Tim backed away, knocking over the length of broom handle that had been leaned against the counter. With all the dust in the air he couldn't be sure, but Bruce thought he smelled the acrid tang of gunpowder rising.

"What's in there, Tim?" he asked.

A scrabbling of claws (or maybe fingernails?) against the wood paneling made Bruce's old heart skip. He snatched the jar of moonshine off the counter and kicked the broom handle out into the foyer.

"Never mind that," Bruce said, "let's just get out of here."

He led Tim by the arm out into the foyer and slide the tall pocket doors closed. As soon as they closed, another scream rang out from inside. Even though it was muffled, it still made Bruce's skin crawl. Tim was barely moving, and Bruce had to shove him out of the way. Tim stumbled and fell to the floor.

"Did you forget how to walk?" Bruce asked. "Give me your hand, I'll pull you up."

Tim slowly raised his hand, and as Bruce hauled him up to his feet, he noticed Tim's mouth was opening and closing repeatedly. At first Bruce thought it was just because the man was scared, but it wasn't until he got closer that he realized Tim was whispering.

He uttered the same word, fear having stolen all tone and inflection from his voice.

"Mom," Tim said. "Mom."

"What about her? Is she here?" Bruce asked, and gave Tim a light slap on the cheek.

Tim nodded as he backpedaled away from the kitchen.

"Shouldn't that be a good thing? You look like you've seen a ghost," Bruce said.

At that, Tim turned and grabbed hold of Bruce's forearm.

"It's not a good thing, no. In fact, it's impossible," he said.

"This world isn't as big as you think it is," Bruce replied.

"No, that's not it. It's impossible because she died when I was a kid."

The sound of something (or someone) crawling out of the dumb waiter was unmistakable. There was a loud crash and a scream, and then more scratching as it made its way across the floor. The pocket doors shook in place as whatever it was crashed against them from the inside.

"That's what I was afraid of," Bruce said, his voice full of despair. "The normal rules don't apply in this house. Nothing is impossible."

The doors stopped shaking and the house fell quiet.

Behind them, the wide double doors to the library began to swing close.

"Guys?"

Bruce turned and saw the doors closing, and Wesley getting up from his post in the corner of the room.

"What's happening?" Tim asked.

Wesley ran toward the rapidly closing doors. "Hey, don't shut me in here!"

"I'm not the one doing it," Bruce said.

Tim, finally coming out of the haze of his shock, grabbed the broom handle and stuck it between the two doors to the library just as they were about to close. The wooden dowel snapped like a twig and the doors slammed shut, Wesley trapped on the inside.

Just as the library doors closed, the kitchen doors flew open with an equally loud crash, followed by an ear-splitting scream. Bruce spun around and saw the woman.

She stood in the doorway between the kitchen and the foyer, staring at them with all white eyes. Her hair floated and swayed all around her as if she was underwater, and her mottled and blue skin glistened in the low light. A wreath of bruises encircled her neck, matching the bruises that peppered her forearms and torso. Her lower stomach was visible through a tear in her shirt. She smiled, and water seeped from the twitching corners of her lips.

"Timmy, is that you?" the woman asked, water spilling out of her mouth in a rush. It splashed onto the floor, spreading out around her in a thin pool.

"Mom?"

"My boy, I've missed you!" the woman cried, throwing her arms open. Her rotting flesh hung low off the bones underneath, water seeping out of scrapes and cuts. "Look at how big you've gotten!"

"Tim, that's not your mother," Bruce warned, but it was too late.

Tim was already across the room and within arm's reach of the woman. She latched onto Tim's shirt and pulled him in for a watery embrace. Then, without moving their feet at all, they floated over the water that had been pooling on the floor and retreated into the kitchen.

"Tim!" Bruce yelled, running toward him, but the pocket doors slid closed as soon as Tim and the woman crossed over the threshold. Unable to stop his momentum, Bruce hit the doors, turning to direct the impact to his shoulder, and ricocheted off to the floor.

The water that had collected on the floor was gone. Bruce rolled and scrambled to his feet, and then rushed to open the door to the kitchen. It wouldn't move at all, as if it had been turned to stone. Bruce pounded on it anyway, but all it managed to do was make his hands hurt.

The stillness of the house around him made the hair on the back of Bruce's neck rise.

Why couldn't he hear Tim?

And what about Wesley?

Bruce rushed to the library doors and found them as immutable as those to the kitchen. The front doors were equally as solid, so he turned in the only direction he had to turn.

Up.

The grand staircase yawned up toward the floors above, where April and John had gone to look for Brady. At the top of the staircase on the first landing stood a figure draped in a white sheet.

Bruce blinked, hoping it was just an illusion, a trick of light and shadow, but the figure did not go away. His heart pounded away in his ribcage, and a lightning bolt of pain shot down his left arm. He winced and placed a hand over his chest.

The figure began to descend the staircase, taking slow and deliberate steps.

Bruce backed up as far as he could, his back pressing against the doors that refused to open, refused to let him escape out into what Ed Bartlett had once called God's field. He didn't dare to move or even blink. He barely even dared to breathe, risking a small sip of air in through his nose.

He caught a scent that made his eyes water, because of the memories the smell triggered.

It was the perfume that Helen wore. He hadn't smelled it since…

"Bruce," she whispered from underneath the sheet that was stamped with *PROPERTY OF MAINE MEDICAL CENTER.* "I'm ready to go home now."

INTERLUDE: PRICE MANOR

What makes a house?

Four sturdy walls, windows, and rooms? A roof to keep out the rain? Trees hewn into lumber, iron into nails, sand into glass, the making of a house is rife with moments of transformation. Even the site where a house is built experiences change, for there now stands a structure where there once was nothing at all.

There is energy in a house, when everything is fresh and new. The energy builds and intensifies as the house becomes something else: a *home*, where people choose to live and go through their own transformations. Houses and homes get to see everything, bear witness to the moments of human existence that range from mirth to madness, and stay behind long after their inhabitants go through their final transformation: from life into death.

Sometimes that final transition happens naturally. Old age, an unfortunate illness. Other times, death happens as result of anger, or the aforementioned madness. The transfer of energy is contained within the walls of the house, where it steeps and becomes stronger.

Price Manor is no different.

Its origins are shrouded in mystery, but it contains an energy so strong, so malevolent that it can transport itself through time, to different parts of the world. It understands the value of transformation, as the house appears different on the inside to every person who mistakenly wanders inside. It understands how to extract the purest form of energy from the prey it seeks, by using some of its own to create monsters and ghouls, bloodthirsty butchers, demonic beings that are expertly skilled at transforming human life into death.

Price Manor is not just a house. It has transformed itself into something close to living, an entity that needs the energy it extracts from others to survive. It is like a magnet, as whenever it picks a new place to land, it draws the unfortunate souls toward it.

But after hundreds upon hundreds of years of hunting, after leaving behind scores of dead in its wake across decades and continents, the power within Price Manor is waning.

Desperate for a place to land, it happened upon an unspoiled hayfield. It used the last of its energy to travel there, and when the dust had settled around it, Price Manor lay still, quiet.

The energy that had lived within it was fully depleted. Gone were the monsters and ghouls, its many halls and vast rooms barren. It was an empty shell, an abandoned house like so many others in this particular time, in this dystopia. Unable to do anything except simply exist, Price Manor remained alone in the field, a worn and battered blight to the landscape.

Waiting.

Even in its hibernation, it knew that even a depleted battery could be recharged.

When a group of six weary travelers sought refuge inside its four walls, it picked up on something within them, not entirely unlike how a shark detects a drop of blood in the ocean.

The house itself may have become exhausted, but each of the six travelers carried demons of their own within.

Price Manor sensed it, could nearly *smell* the blood which would soon be flowing.

For as human life transformed into death, as blood seeped into the dry floorboards or spattered upon the rose-patterned wallpaper, it would breathe new life into the walls of this particular house.

So, instead of conjuring monsters of its own, Price Manor let the minds of its current inhabitants do the heavy lifting. And in doing so, it silently answered a question:

What is inside an abandoned house?

Only what you bring in with you.

The sleeping house awakens, eager to consume, to build up its strength, to sup on the fear and abject terror that will soon run rampant through its halls. Even though it had become tired, that did not negate its thirst.

And Price Manor slakes its thirst with blood and fear and death.

WESLEY

As someone who had spent his fair share of time in enclosed spaces, Wesley typically didn't suffer from claustrophobia. On the contrary, he found some sort of comfort in a confined space. Between his various stints in prison and psychiatric hospitals over the last three decades, he had likely spent more time in confinement than as a free man.

Being stuck in this library, however, was something else entirely.

Wesley paced around the room, trying not to let his emotions get out of control. If he got too heightened he'd have to take one of his pills, but he couldn't really afford it. His supply was dangerously low, and if he could just control his breathing, he'd be okay.

He stormed past the doors to the foyer, which might as well have been stone, as it would not move even the slightest amount. He had given up on trying to get them open, as all he managed to do was strain his muscles.

"Christ, what I wouldn't give for a stiff drink right now," he said to the empty room.

He walked around a couch and tripped on the corner of an area rug that had flipped up and caught on his sneaker. Wesley fell forward onto his knees, and the change in perspective allowed him to see an object under the couch that was closest to the library doors.

It was a glass jar, and it was half-filled with a clear liquid.

Wesley smiled. "Ask and ye shall receive."

He had spent enough time in backwoods Maine mobile homes to know there was only one kind of clear liquid you stored in Mason jars. Wesley crawled over to the couch and stuck his arm underneath to fish it out. All it took was a whiff of the contents to confirm: it was moonshine.

Wesley sat on the floor, his back against the couch, and took a few swallows. It was harsh stuff, but he had drank far more stringent stuff in prison. He waited a few minutes for the alcohol to do its job, the warmth of it already beginning to spread, and set about figuring out how he was going to escape.

He had done a lot of that, as an inmate or an inpatient, and he had a few tricks up his sleeve.

The room spun when Wesley stood up. He hadn't gotten good and drunk in a while (it was a bad idea while on prescription antipsychotics), and forgotten how good it felt.

"That is some good shit," he said to himself, and made sure to put the lid on the jar. He set it on an end table and surveyed the room with fresh eyes. All of a sudden, the concept of him being trapped inside of a library became absolutely preposterous.

Wesley broke out in laughter. The sound filled the room, but it sounded foreign to him. Like a crazy person. Like the Joker from those Batman movies.

"It was the Colonel, in the library, with the rope!" he cried. This struck him as even more funny, which drew more laughter. "No, it was the guy with latent psychopathic tendencies, in the grocery store, with the knife!"

Wesley collapsed to the floor in a fit of laughter, but the laughter soon changed into crying. He couldn't deny it to himself anymore. He was scared, because there was something wrong with this house. He had been a skeptic before, but now he knew.

He had to get out of here, but how?

The windows, maybe?

Wesley clumsily got to his feet and wove his way over to one of the windows. He tried to pry it open but when that didn't work, he grabbed a lamp off a side table, and threw it at the glass. The lamp bounced off, breaking into several pieces. He picked up the base of the lamp and smashed it repeatedly against the glass, but it did not give.

His eyes became bleary with sweat, and when he wiped them with his hands, the window suddenly had bars over them. They looked just like the ones that covered the lone window in his cell at Spring Meadow.

"What the fuck is wrong with this place?" he wondered, and wiped off the sweat that had cropped up on his forehead, as well.

The windows were clearly a no go. The room to the opposite side of the library that Wesley thought Brady had run off to also yielded no options. There were no doors to other rooms on the inside, nor any windows.

Defeated, Wesley turned to face the wall that was lined with bookcases.

Anyone who gave a shit about books would have loved this space, but Wesley couldn't care less. He was quite literate but found reading to be boring, but as his eyes roved over the exposed spines, an idea struck him.

Maybe there's a secret passage way, he thought. He thought back to a movie he had watched while being held captive in the looney bin. Some rich billionaire had a massive library just like this one in his opulent mansion, and there was a mechanism attached to one of the books that made one of the bookcases swing out to reveal a hidden room tucked away behind it.

Given how grand this house appeared to be, Wesley thought there was a good chance that he'd find one here.

He scrambled across the room, tearing books off the shelves with both hands. Books cascaded down, a waterfall of titles and author names. One hand added books by Salt, Gloom, Goodwin, Stewart, and Newlin into the heap on the floor, the other hauled down the spines of Brocklehurst, Hamilton, Pennington, and Eliot. Wesley trampled these books underfoot, not caring about how he was damaging them, leaving behind a trail of bent covers and torn pages in his wake.

Wesley worked his way down the wall, clearing every shelf from top to bottom, finding that none of them were attached to anything that opened the escape route he so desperately wanted. He came upon his pistol and tossed it carelessly aside along with all of the discarded books.

The icy tendrils of claustrophobia were starting to creep in, threatening his tenuous grip on his anxiety. When he reached the last shelf and no hidden door had revealed itself, Wesley's desperation had reached a fever pitch. Sweat poured down his face, and he grunted with the effort of clearing the last shelf.

He had become dependent on the idea that this was going to be his way to freedom. He needed this to work, a stringent requirement in the same way that he needed oxygen to breathe. There was one last grouping of books on a chest-high shelf, and with a weary, defeated sigh, he grabbed them and tore them down.

All but one of them tumbled down, a single hardback remained in place.

Hope leapt into Wesley's throat. He kicked the books on the floor out of his way and looked more closely at the one that was left behind. He tilted his head to the side so he could read the title.

THE LIFE AND DEATH OF CLIVE WESLEY.

His breath hitched, and Wesley blinked to make sure he was seeing things clearly. The gray cloth that wrapped around the hardback looked old, faded by age and exposure to sunlight.

It must be about some other guy with the same name, Wesley thought. *It can't be about me. That'd be impossible.*

Wesley reached for the book, his hand trembling. This time, the book came away from the shelf freely, and as he lifted it away he heard a soft *click*. The bookshelf shuddered and popped away from the wall but only by a small degree. There were too many books on the floor impeding it from swinging out any further.

But all Wesley could focus on was the book in his hand.

The front cover repeated the title in an elaborate font, inlaid in gold leaf. It also bore the author's name.

V. Price

A shiver traced up his back as he recalled seeing the same surname in the stonework as he walked under the archway and into the house just a few hours before. Unable to resist, he opened the cover and turned to the first page.

Clive Wesley began his life alone in an alley on Pine Street in Lewiston, Maine on August 31ˢᵗ, 1991. His mother (name unknown) left him in a cardboard box, still attached to the placenta. A passing police officer heard the sound of a baby crying and went to investigate. Upon finding the newborn, the officer could not believe his luck.

63

Instead of bringing the child to the hospital and filing the requisite paperwork, the policeman brought the child home to his wife. She was unable to bear a child of her own, and the sadness that he saw in her was too much to bear. This child was clearly unwanted by his mother, and Officer Wesley knew his wife would love this child as her own.

Wesley continued reading, breathless at the impossibility that this book contained the story of his life. His parents had never revealed that they weren't his birth parents, but it didn't take a geneticist to see that. He didn't resemble either of them in the slightest, and there was no clear genetic markers like eye or hair color that had been passed down to him.

He flipped through the pages, seeing his entire life documented in exquisite detail. His first romantic relationship (that went horribly wrong), his most secret fetishes which he had never uttered to anyone, his inner most thoughts that had no reason being written in the book he held in his hands. It was like the author had been in his mind, taking notes his entire life, leaving him with no privacy, documenting all of his secrets and publishing it in this book.

Anger bubbled up at the violation of his privacy, and that anyone could have picked up this book and read these things about them. Maybe they already had, and that was why they had locked him inside this room alone. Wesley wanted to throw the book across the room, wanted to set it on fire, wanted to find that *V. Price* guy and throttle him.

Maybe even stab him a little.

This book knew how everything began, including how he managed to escape from Spring Meadow (and how many people he killed to achieve his freedom), surviving in a world that was vastly different than it was when he was incarcerated (and how many people he killed to ensure his continued survival), and then joining up with the group. Everything was accurate and quite detailed, including to the point where he entered this damn house.

As he continued to read, his eyes fell on the page header and he was reminded of the title.

THE LIFE AND DEATH OF CLIVE WESLEY.

There was only a few pages left in the book. Did that mean…

"No," he said, clapping the book closed. "Just… no."

His entire body trembled, unable to process what was happening. He pinched himself to make sure he wasn't dreaming, and then felt a cool wind circle around his ankles.

That was when Wesley remembered that the bookshelf had moved. He tucked the book under his arm and pulled on the bookshelf, yanking it away from the wall. The mountain of books on the floor blocked its path, so Wesley kicked and pushed them out of the way. At last there was enough room and the bookshelf swung wide, revealing a stone staircase that descended into an endless dark.

Wesley looked back at the library, now completely disheveled, and considered if going into the basement was a better choice than just staying put. He had been hoping for another room, perhaps a stairway that led *up*stairs instead of further down, so that he could find a way to get out of this house. There was a possibility that there were other means of egress from the basement, but there was only one way to find out.

He ran back to grab his pack, stuffing the book that contained the story of his life inside. He wasn't sure if he would be coming back, and didn't want to leave it behind. Then, without much other thought or consideration, stepped down onto the first basement step.

Before he could turn around, the bookcase began to swing closed. Wesley tried to hold it open, but whatever force was pushing it closed was too strong. The dim light the windows offered that had spilled down into the stairway was squeezed out, and Wesley scrambled for his flashlight. He managed to switch it on just as the door met the wall. A latch somewhere in the bookcase made a *clunk*, and Wesley understood that there was no going back, not even if he wanted to. Aiming the flashlight down the stairs, he took each step carefully and soon reached the bottom.

As he swung the flashlight around, Wesley saw that the space was not as big as he imagined it would be. It was quite small, in fact. It reminded him of his room at Spring Meadow. There was even a small cot in the same corner as where his bed was, and a desk in the opposing corner, same as where he used to write his journal. There was even a half bathroom that had the same pedestal sink…

The similarities were uncanny. Wesley's brain churned, realizing with incredulity that this was an exact recreation of his room at the psych ward, covered in a layer of dust and cobwebs.

"There's no way…" Wesley began, but was unable to finish. He had turned back toward the stone stairway and found it was gone, replaced by a solid steel door. It was *his* door, Wesley knew, because he had spent so much time staring at it. He would have recognized it anywhere.

It was the door to his cell at the hospital, which completed the elaborate set that had been created for him. It bore the same scratches and scuffs left behind by decades of being kicked open and closed, but what made it truly authentic was the etching in the top corner.

Charles Adler was here.

Wesley had asked around about a patient with that name, and learned he had killed himself years before. He killed a pregnant woman and her young child while driving drunk, and was admitted after being diagnosed clinically insane. The fact that Wesley shared a room with a murderer didn't bother him; in fact it made him feel more welcomed.

Wesley sat down on the bed, his backpack slipping off his shoulder. Something fell out of an open pocket and spun away on the rough stone floor. He pointed his flashlight toward it and saw it was the book, the one that supposedly knew how he was going to die.

Motes of dust floated in the beam of light. Wesley had every intention of leaving the book there, maybe even using the pages for toilet paper for when nature called. He jumped when the cover flipped open and the pages began to turn over. Then, the book slid back across the floor toward him. It was left open to one of the last few pages. He followed it instinctively with the flashlight, and his eyes went to the top of the page.

On the night of his death, Wesley sat on the bed, reading his book when there was a knock on the door.

A scream tore out of his mouth when two heavy knocks came from the other side of the steel door. It was involuntary, his nerves balanced on a razor's edge.

The door swung open, and Wesley's immediately recognized his visitor.

It was true. Wesley never forgot the face of the first man he killed, the unlucky man in the supermarket bread aisle.

"Remember me?" the man said, pressing both of his hands against his abdomen. Wesley found himself without words, his mouth hanging open. "It's okay, it was a rhetorical question."

The man looked at the book laying open on the floor and bent to pick it up. Something dripped off his hand onto the floor, and left a dark stain on the cloth binding.

"Don't let me interrupt your reading," the man said, tossing the book onto Wesley's lap. "Go on, I think you're just getting to the good part."

APRIL

April rounded the corner and came upon a hallway that was lined with doors, and it seemed to go on forever. Darkness shrouded everything, her flashlight giving her only a narrow view of what lay ahead. April had heard a door close somewhere down here, that much she knew. That meant Brady was in one of these rooms, and the sooner she found him, the sooner they could all go back to sleep.

She followed the sound down the hallway and around the corner, unaware that at some point, she had lost John. April had forgotten about him nearly completely, in the deserted hallway that trailed behind her.

Her flashlight caught on a set of footprints that led down the endless hallway. They were clear, as if they had been pressed intentionally into the dust that lay like a carpet over the hardwood floor. April slowed her steps so she could look at one more closely. The pattern of the footprint was distinct, and one she recognized. The telltale crosshatching of Vans wouldn't be one she'd soon forget.

She first saw the footprints outside her windows. They trampled over the sparse garden she had planted, and she instinctively took pictures of them with her phone. Later, she would email them to the detective she had spoken to about establishing a restraining order.

Dustin always wore Vans, even to work. She knew this about him, because he was proud of his

69

sneaker collection. It was one of the things he would often talk about at length, and to anyone who would listen.

Her heart skipped, until she reminded herself that there was no possibility that those tracks could have been made by her former stalker. When he showed up on her doorstep, ready to do whatever harm he had planned, April had pulled the trigger enough times to guarantee that he wouldn't get up again. Surely these footprints were left by Brady. It made the most sense, and it would explain the sound of the door closing down the hall.

April shook her head, as if that would physically remove the worried thoughts and nervousness that threatened her resolve. If convincing herself that everything was fine didn't work, tightening her grip on her pistol certainly helped. There wasn't much she had reason to be afraid of, so long as she had a few rounds left in the magazine.

She continued down the hall, following the footprints in the dust. The hallway stretched out before her, and April followed the trail intently, losing track of time and of how far she had walked. She realized that something was amiss when her feet began to hurt, and that she was in desperate need of a drink of water.

April paused in the middle of the hallway, and realized she hadn't heard John speak a single word in quite some time. This was unusual, as he could be a chatterbox when nervous. She turned and was shocked to find she was alone in the hallway.

"John?" she called out.

There was no response, not even an echo.

As she swung her flashlight back around, it highlighted something on the floor that made her breath catch in her throat.

The footprints. They diverged in many different directions from exactly where she stood. There were at least a dozen doors within eyesight, six on each side of the hall, and there were Vans footprints leading toward each door. None of them showed tracks retreating.

How could that be?

"Brady, if you can hear me, it's time to cut the shit," April said, forcing an edge into her voice.

Behind her, a door opened and closed. April whirled around but was too late. A swirl of dust on the floor told her which door it was, but when she tried to open it, the knob wouldn't turn. Another door opened and slammed shut, again from behind. The noise made her jump, her flashlight starting to jitter in her hand.

And then at once, all of the doors in the hallway began to open and shut repeatedly, slamming into their frames with such force that it made the entire hallway shake and tremble. The noise was deafening.

Helpless, she spun around in a circle, watching as the doors around her swung open and closed. She saw a split-second glimpse into one of the rooms and saw a man being consumed by a ravenous beast. The beast turned to look at April, its eyes burning black. The man was screaming, bleeding from his eyes and from the gouges in his torso and arms, but the sound of the doors slamming in the hall drowned him out. The door closed on this horror scene as April continued around turning.

In another room, she saw a roof nearly full to the ceiling with water, and a woman suspended within it, struggling to reach the surface. Her hair was a tangled corona around her entire face, a flurry of bubbles

71

erupting from her mouth. A tentacle reached up from the dark depths and wrapped around her ankle, pulling her down. The door closed, and April turned.

In the next, she saw Brady. He was standing in the middle of the room that was off the library, yet somehow that room was now upstairs. He was wrapped in a corpse's embrace, bones wrapped in a decaying blouse pressing into his back. Together, they were sinking into the ground, as the floor had been pulled back, revealing an open grave that was ready to receive them both. The door closed, and April turned.

Each door showed her a new and horrible scene. A man drowning in blood. A tall figure in a grotesque smiley-face mask using a sickle to split open the neck of a man who looks like a carny. A deranged man with a paring knife, peeling strips of his own skin off his legs and eating it. A roaring fireplace, flames engulfed around a man sitting deep within. A tangle of rotting corpses, gyrating as if it were an orgy, ravenously devouring a man caught in the middle. A woman appearing to apply lipstick, except the lipstick tube was a shard of glass and she was slashing her lips to ribbons. April kept turning away, but everywhere she looked there was only scenes of death.

At last April realized she could stop turning. She willed her feet to stop moving and crouched down in the hallway, closing her eyes. The doors continued to open and close, the vibrations making her dizzy, and she screamed.

The scream rose above all the noise, and the doors stopped all at once.

The absence of sound left April's ears ringing. She stood and looked around her, hoping that all of the doors had been left closed, letting a sigh of relief out after confirming they were.

She was overwhelmed by a sense of fear and nostalgia, and wondered if that was what she had just witnessed. Had all of those people died in this house? Was each room playing back the scene of their death, like a macabre highlight reel?

April immediately thought of Brady, and what she had seen of him. Did that mean that he was dead?

She didn't have much time to think, as behind her, a single door opened. It creaked ominously as it swung. April knew she had to turn, had to see what was waiting for her, but she was too frightened. She looked down at her hands, and remembered that she was holding her pistol. What was there to be afraid of, with a dozen lead projectiles at the ready? A grim smile erased the fear she felt and she spun around.

"Fancy seeing you here," Dustin said, looming in the doorway. Blossoms of red stained his shirt, from where she had shot him the first time. His skin was pallid and green, hanging loose off his cheeks.

"You can't be here," April said. "That's impossible."

"Love conquers all things," Dustin replied. "Even the impossible."

He staggered out of the doorway toward April.

April backpedaled, raising her pistol level with Dustin's chest. *Déjà vu* washed over her, as she had done this once already and thought that once had been enough.

It *should* have been enough.

April squeezed the trigger.

The muzzle flash lit up the hallway orange and yellow, the bullet striking Dustin squarely in the chest.

He shuddered as it passed through him, tearing out shreds of his heart and lungs and spattering them against the wall behind him. Dustin only grunted and took another step forward.

She pulled the trigger again, and again. The sound of gunfire made her ears ring, but she remained focused on the aberration that stood before her. The rounds struck him in his torso and abdomen, just as they had before, but this time, he did not drop to the floor. Instead of blood issuing from the entry wounds, black sludge seeped out in thick driblets.

"You're going to have to try harder than that," Dustin coughed, more of the black goop coming out of his mouth as he spoke.

April understood there was no value in wasting the rest of her ammunition, which was in precious short supply, but raised her pistol a little higher and squeezed off one last shot. This one struck him in the center of his forehead. A dark hole appeared and his head rocked back, a sickening snap coming from his neck as it broke. His head rolled limp to one side, and laughter coming from his perforated lungs forced out showers of blood and gore from his drooping mouth.

Dustin used one hand to push his head back into place, but without an intact neck to support the weight of his skull, it toppled forward. Bone ground against bone as his chin dropped to his chest, and he used both hands to lift and hold his head in the proper position so he could see her.

April cringed and holstered her pistol. If a headshot wasn't going to work, she wasn't sure what would, and she was running out of options.

"John?" she called out, desperate for backup.

Dustin laughed. "I don't think he's going to be much help."

"Why, what did you do?" April thought for a moment. "What did this *house* do?"

"Maybe one of these doors will tell you," Dustin suggested, pointing behind her. "Go ahead, take a look."

April thought if one of the doors contained something she could tolerate more than the decomposing, limp-necked reanimated corpse of her stalker, she would take it.

Dustin took another lurching step forward, holding his head in place as it wobbled on the broken stump of his spine. April juked to the left, hoping he would take the bait. He did, and when she pulled back and to the right, she grinned as he fell face-first onto the floor. April grabbed for the first door that was closest to her and pushed it open.

John was on the other side, standing in the hallway just around the corner from the first floor landing. The lower half of his calves were sunken into the floor and he looked up at April, his face stricken with fear.

"April, help me," he gasped.

She had never seen the big man seem so helpless, so afraid... and then she saw what was pulling him down into the floor.

It was a woman, covered in lesions that seeped a milky fluid. The muscles in her arms rippled as she held strong onto John's legs, pulling him down. The woman's hair, tight curls weighed down with sweat and the sticky mess that issued from her lesions, hung over her face.

And yet April thought she recognized her. John had shown her a picture of her once.

The woman snapped her head back, revealing a face covered in festering sores, but it confirmed April's suspicions. It was Amanda, John's deceased wife.

"Come back, John," the woman was hissing, "The kids and I miss you so much."

April looked on as John continued to struggle, hands scrabbling against the hardwood floor for purchase and finding none. Two small, shrouded figures crawled out from under the floorboards on Amanda's back, clinging to her ragged clothing.

"Come back home, Daddy," one of them said, his voice garbled by water that spilled out of his mouth. His skin also covered in lesions, and his flesh was bloated.

"We miss you so much, Daddy," the other one chimed in, her voice also muted by the waterfall that tumbled over her lips.

Both of the dead children crawled further up to get closer to John. One grabbed hold of his belt, the other his backpack, and together they all pulled him back.

Stunned by what she was seeing, April realized she had to do something to help. She reached for her pistol, wondering if it would be more effective against them than Dustin, but the door slammed closed in front of her.

She felt his fetid breath on her neck and knew he was close, too close for comfort.

"I'm sure he'll be fine," Dustin said from behind her. "Or he won't. Either way, his fate is his own to decide, as is yours."

April felt a pinch on the back of her neck, and then everything went black.

TIM

The kitchen doors closed behind him, and suddenly Tim realized that everything was wrong.

He planted his feet on the floor, but the pool of water that had collected made the tile slick underfoot. Sand and silt added some grit, but it wasn't enough.

The sound of water rushing over stones cut through his fear and Tim looked up to see, inexplicably, the brook that had been across the street from his childhood home, right in the middle of the kitchen.

It hurt something in his mind, something deep within, to see the river running through the tile and cabinetry. It was wrong, out of place, to see something from his memories presented here, in this place. There was that, and Tim had never seen the water this high. It crested over the rocks that lined the edges of the brook, set perfectly in the tile, as the current surged through, splashing up and spraying him. It had grown dark, and all along the far side of the brook were pairs of white and green (and sometimes red) eyes of the predators that lay in wait.

"Do you remember this place?" his mother asked.

Tim shuddered as he felt her cold hand caress his cheek. "Runoff River," he replied.

His mother chuckled, the sound like more water over rocks.

"And do you remember the summer I died? You thought there was some animal across the street, making all of those horrible screaming noises?"

He nodded.

"You thought it was an owl," she mused, "Only it wasn't an owl after all. It was me, screaming at the hands of your father."

She spun Tim around so they were face to face. He hadn't wanted to see her this close, didn't want to see how ugly and purple the bruises around her neck were, how battered and beaten her upper arms and stomach were. She noticed him taking stock of her injuries, and chuckled some more.

"Your father always made sure to leave his marks where they could be covered up. He couldn't have anyone asking questions or sticking their nose into our business," she said. "I suppose if he hadn't killed me, I would have had to wear turtlenecks for a while."

At this she laughed, leaning her head back to cackle at the vaulted ceiling. It was a sound that made Tim feel like he would go insane if he had to listen to it for one more second. He tried covering his ears, but that wasn't enough.

He clamped a hand over his mother's mouth.

Her slick skin and wrinkled lips felt horrid under his palm, but the laughter stopped. His mother slapped his hand away, hard.

"Taking a page out of your father's playbook, are you?" she spat.

"No, it's not like that. I was—"

"Trying to keep me quiet. Just like your father."

She wheeled back and slapped him again, water spraying out of her bloated skin. Tim stumbled back, nearly falling into the river.

"You want to know what it was like, being beaten by him?" she asked.

"No, I'm sure it was horrible, Mom," Tim began. "I'm sorry I didn't notice, but what could I have done? I was a child."

"You could have done *something*," she hissed. "You could have told someone that things didn't feel right at home, that you wanted nothing to do but hide in your room, away from all the fighting."

This struck a chord within him, as this was something Tim had thought obsessively about in the decades since this happened. He shouldered some of the blame, a misplaced burden of guilt at not being able to protect his mother, of not being strong enough to defy his father's strong hand, even if it never landed upon him.

"You were such a weak child, who clearly grew up to become a weak man. What would your father think of you, if he could see you now?"

Tim winced at his mother's words. He often wondered how he'd stack up to his father's scrutiny, which was part of what pushed him to succeed in his adult life, though no achievement ever felt good enough.

"I think he'd be proud," Tim managed, his voice weak.

"You'd be wrong," said a raspy voice from the shadows across the river.

His father stepped out from the brush and trees that had hidden him. He was missing the top two thirds of his face, just like he was the last time Tim had seen him. In his hands was the shotgun he had used to end his life. He racked the pump to eject the spent shell and load in a fresh one.

"You were supposed to be dead, Margaret," he continued.

Tim scrambled to his feet as his father leveled the shotgun at his mother, holding it at the hip. How his father knew where she was standing was beyond Tim's understanding, because he had no eyes left in his skull.

"She is dead, and so are you!" Tim yelled. "You killed her and then killed yourself, leaving me to be an orphan. Do you know what that was like? You might as well have killed me, too!"

Tim wiped away hot, angry tears and stood in front of the barrel, in front of his mother.

"To get her, you'll have to go through me," Tim said.

Then, out of the corner of his eye, Tim saw something floating down the river. It was flat and white, and it spun in circles as it bounced off of the stones Tim had once used to hop across to the other side. It careened off a half-sunken branch and came to a stop at his feet, docking itself on a rock on the river's edge.

It was the envelope his father had left for him before he blew his head off when Tim was a child. Tim had left it behind, and when offered it by a social worker later on, he refused. That was another regret of his, but he knew it wouldn't have changed anything even if he had read it. His mother would still be dead, killed by his father. His father would still be dead, unwilling to face the consequences of his actions. Not knowing what his father's last words to him were sometimes weighed on him, but that envelope had gotten lost ages ago. Now, Tim stared at it, resting at his feet.

"You going to open it this time, Timmy?" his father asked. "Or are you going to be a coward?"

Tim looked up.

"I am many things, but I am *not* a coward," he said.

Tim lunged at his father, propelled by anger that had been within him for decades.

And the shotgun roared.

Tim fell short, the blast of lead from the shotgun catching him in the stomach. He twisted midair and fell into the river.

The water was cold, comforting. It crested over him, pulling threads of blood from him and washing them away. Tim rolled his eyes up to where his father had stood and saw that he was gone, replaced by a tree trunk that had been broken off. It was draped in red vines, and a branch jutted out at one side.

The tree vaguely resembled a human form, perhaps enhanced by shadow and fear. Tim looked over to where his mother had stood. She had been replaced by a weeping willow tree, and it was shedding its leaves like tears.

A breeze caught some of the leaves and carried them to river, where they floated down and around Tim. He could feel himself weakening, losing control of his consciousness. He wondered what had struck him, then, for if his father hadn't been real, the shotgun mustn't been real, either.

The injuries to his abdomen, however, were very real, and very dire.

Unable to move, Tim explored his wounds with his fingers. There were several entry points, more than he could count in his fading mind. His fingers became sticky with blood as he felt gingerly around them, and then felt something sticking out from one of the wounds.

He grasped onto it and pulled, grunting at the pain it caused. He lifted it up and held it in front of his face, blinking to focus his eyes in the lowering light.

It was a shred of paper. Smeared by his blood, Tim could barely discern his father's handwriting.

... e you, son...

Tim let his arm fall back into the water. The current tugged the remnant of his father's suicide note out of his grasp and it wheeled away downstream, gone forever.

What had he written? A word ending in *E*, followed by *"you, son"*.

Love ended with an *E*.

So did *hate*.

Reading his father's words did exactly what Tim suspected they would, and changed nothing.

Tim closed his eyes. He was tired, so very tired, and the water had begun whispering to him a lullaby that he could not ignore. It made him forget that he was alone, abandoned, like he had felt for most of his life. It made him forget that he was dying.

The current of the river rocked him gently into forever sleep.

JOHN

The moment he recognized his deceased wife crawling on top of him, John knew something was terribly wrong. His first thought was that he was hallucinating, that he had some sort of catastrophic mental break, but no.

She was here, and she was very much dead.

A strangled noise of fear and effort came from him as he pushed her off and away. As much as he missed his wife, this was not the reunion he had hoped for. He planted a foot in her chest and kicked the same way he would have kicked a door down in a burning building, and she flew backwards.

John got to his feet, breathing hard, and made it only a few paces down the hall before another hole in the floorboards appeared, too suddenly for him to avoid stepping in it. He fell in, and felt the bones in his shin snap. John bellowed in pain.

"Where are you going, John?" Amanda said from behind him. Her voice was wrong, not hers yet unmistakably hers at the same time.

"You're not my wife," John managed through clenched teeth. He turned around and pulled his ruined leg out of the hole. The jagged edges of his tibia and fibula protruded out of both his skin and his pant leg. He didn't need medical training to know that this was bad. Very bad.

"Of course I am," she purred, slithering closer. The lesions that covered her skin oozed and dripped, leaving hissing scorch marks on the floor in her wake.

83

"I've been waiting for you to come back home. Come with me, I'll show you the way."

She extended a hand, more bone than flesh. Maggots wriggled out from under a flap of skin.

To this, John rolled back around and tried to crawl away. He wasn't sure what was going on, knew that none of this could possibly be real, but the horrible pit in his stomach told him it was. He used his arms to pull him forward, and felt the wet pressure of a hand on the back of his good leg.

"Don't you want to see the kids?" she asked. "Don't you miss them?"

She pulled John back as if he weighed nothing, until his good leg hung over the hole in the floor. She pushed down, breaking it, and John screamed again.

Adrenaline and instinct took control, and somehow John found the strength to pull himself away just a few feet just as the hole in the floor widened.

Then, a door to his right opened, revealing a frightened-looking April.

"April, help me," John gasped.

"Come back, John," Amanda hissed, "The kids and I miss you so much."

John scrabbled against the hardwood floor, his hands failing to grab on anything that he could pull himself away with. He heard a noise from behind him. It sounded like something else had crawled out from under the floor.

"Come back home, Daddy," a small, wet voice said.

"We miss you so much, Daddy," said another.

John closed his eyes, knowing that his children had come to join him.

He felt them crawl onto him, a sensation that was oddly nostalgic and terrifying at the same time. He remembered them crawling on him after they tackled him to the floor once he arrived home from work, but it had never been quite like this. For starters, the last time they had done that, they had both been alive.

John raised his head to plead to April once more, and saw someone standing behind her that he did not recognize. He barely had time to wonder who the mystery man was when the door slammed closed.

Julian grabbed hold of his belt, and Emily stripped him of his backpack. Together with Amanda, they dragged him back. John shuddered, wishing desperately for his exhausted body to produce more adrenaline to numb the incredible pain he felt in his shattered legs, to give him more energy to fight back.

But he had nothing more to give. The one thing he always had to fall back on, his innate athletic endurance, had finally worn out, and at the one time in his life he needed it the most.

John rolled onto his back and closed his eyes, feeling the bloated, tiny fingers of Julian and Emily pull against his clothing. They tore at the fabric, exposing his chest, his thighs, his arms.

The children began chattering in a language that made John's eardrums feel like they were going to burst. Not because it was loud, but because it sounded like something not meant for mortals, a language spoken only by the makers and doers of evil. Amanda barked a command in the same tongue, and the children fell quiet.

John opened his eyes and saw the three of them standing over him. The glow from his forgotten flashlight under-lit their faces, giving them an even more ghoulish appearance.

His dead wife grunted another command, and John watched as his two dead children moved in complete unison. They used their fingertips to rip open the boils and sores on their skin, dripping the pus and disease onto John's bare skin.

It burned into him as if it were acid, spreading across his body. John bit down on his lips to keep his mouth closed despite the scream that wanted to tear out of him, for fear of the sickening fluid entering his mouth.

"Now you're just like us, Daddy," Emily said.

Julian giggled, a sound John at one point would have given nearly anything to hear one last time, except now it made John tremble.

"Yeah, now you're *dead*!" Julian exclaimed, as if this was a prize won at the fair. "You're dead! You're dead!"

The disease that they had given him was quickly devouring his skin and the muscles underneath. The pain was tremendous, eclipsing that of his broken legs. It burned straight through him, right down to the floorboards as the children continued to sprinkle the disease that brought an end to human civilization across the rest of him. He felt it on his eyes now, his cheeks, and then at last, his mouth.

As his lips burned through, revealing a skeleton's smile, Amanda grunted and the children fell back. John was losing his grip on consciousness. He felt the void of the beyond looming above him like a black hole, and all he wanted to do was fall in.

John breathed his last and was dragged away in the clutches of his dead children.

BRUCE

Oddly enough, Bruce was not afraid.

He had seen much in his life, and the scale on which he judged things had changed through its duration, especially when it came to determining what he was most afraid of. As a child, it was seeing his brother stricken with a fever and wondering if he was going to die. As a teenager, it was summoning the courage to ask Helen Conrad to the junior prom. As a new recruit, it was staring at the enemy through his rifle sights and trying to hold the barrel steady.

Fear, he determined, was relative.

So when his deceased wife appeared in the foyer, it was not fear that he felt. Instead, it was something like relief.

"Did you hear me, Bruce?" Helen asked, advancing even closer to him. Close enough for him to detect another smell that had first been hidden by her perfume.

It was the smell of decay, of filth, of waste. It was the way the entire hospital smelled the day he had brought Helen in to be seen by her physician. No amount of industrial-grade disinfectant or air fresheners could cover the smell of hundreds of patients rotting in their beds, in the hallways, in the waiting rooms. The disease that toppled the country Bruce once fought for was cruel, harsh, and when it hit Maine, it hit hard.

Bruce had felt the quickening of his heart when the front doors to Maine Medical Center slid open and the sound of chaos and the smell of death slammed into him like a wall. Helen's sense of smell had diminished years before, so she had asked him if he was alright when he hesitated before rolling her wheelchair inside. He wasn't afraid of going in, but this affront gave him pause.

"Yes," he had said, lying. "I'm fine, just catching my breath. Pushing you around is hard work."

He could tell she had smiled, even under her paper surgical mask. She always smiled more with her eyes than anything else, and they had twinkled at him then. They had a long history of razzing each other, and even though the situation with her health had become dire, he knew if he starting treating her differently, she would chastise him for it.

"That's because you're a tired, old man," she replied with a cough. "Now let's get moving. I don't want to be late."

They proceeded into the hospital and made their way through the halls, up an elevator, around a few corners, and then finally into the Geriatric Medicine wing. By then, Bruce was truly in need of a break, silently cursing the hospital for making the Old Folks Department (as he called it) so far away from the entrance.

Due to the new illness going around, Bruce wasn't allowed into the exam room with Helen, despite much protest. He was relegated to the waiting room with the other outcasts, with nothing but outdated magazines and the incessant drone of the local news on a wall-mounted TV to pass the time.

Lots of people were scared by the news, but Bruce wasn't one of them. He thought it was dramatized hyperbole, all this talk about the potential of "drastic measures" to contain the spread, military-enforced quarantines due to all of the civil unrest. This was all things you saw happen in other states, in much bigger cities. Not in Maine, where there were more trees than people.

The wait time was extended, and Bruce unknowingly fell asleep in his chair. He was roused by someone repeatedly calling his name, which sounded at first like it was coming from a great distance. With great effort he sat up in his chair and blinked away the unexpected sleep from his eyes.

"Bruce Gentry?" A nurse wearing a disposable sterile suit and a plastic face shield stood waiting impatiently in front of the double doors that led on to the exam rooms.

"Coming," he grunted and heaved himself out of his chair.

They were a few paces down the hall past the doors before he asked.

"How is she looking?"

The nurse refused to meet his eyes, which told Bruce all he needed to know.

"The doctor will explain everything to you," she replied, and then pointed to a door to one side of the hall. "Right here."

Helen was laying on a bed, her body draped in a white sheet from the chest down. An oxygen mask was strapped to her face, and a tangle of wires snaked down from under the sheet to a rack of monitors and machines. A thin man, wearing the same protective gear as the nurse, stood at a computer in the corner, typing.

"What happened?" he demanded.

The man turned to Bruce and cleared his throat.

"Mr. Gentry, I'm Dr. Lewis. Ordinarily I'd offer to shake hands, but under the circumstances, I think we'll forgo the formalities and get down to it."

Bruce nodded his agreement, and the doctor continued.

"I apologize to be the bearer of bad news, but your wife… She fell unconscious during her check-up. There was a point where her heart stopped, but we were able to revive her. She's stable now, but she is still unconscious, and I'm afraid she doesn't have much time left."

Bruce went to his wife's side, and the nurse stopped him short.

"I'm sorry, but she's infected," she said.

He had half a mind to toss the nurse out of his way, but suddenly he didn't feel like he was capable of remaining on his feet. Bruce fell into a nearby chair.

The doctor took a step closer to Bruce, still observing a cautious distance.

"When you are ready, we need to talk about hospice," he said gently.

The room spun, but Bruce willed it to stop. He sat up in his chair and shook his head.

"No, she was fine. She was a bit under the weather, sure, but she was fine when we came in here. I don't know what you quacks did to her, but there's no way she's…"

He trailed off.

They had been careful not to expose themselves to any risks when word of the latest illness came about. The coronavirus had been bad enough back in 2020 and they had dodged the bullet then, and had managed to do so again now.

Or so Bruce thought.

Helen had gone out to play cards one night about a week ago. She hadn't felt well since, but Bruce had been distracted with making repairs to their furnace in preparation for the cold weather that was just around the corner.

"I'm sorry," he said. "I just didn't know. She was always good at hiding that kind of thing."

"We'll need to examine you, and take a few tests to see if you're infected, as well," Dr. Lewis said. "I hope you understand. It's just a precaution."

Bruce stood up and shook his head.

"No. Absolutely not."

The doctor reached out to put a hand on his shoulder, but Bruce swatted it away.

"Don't touch me!" Bruce said. "You can't do anything without my consent. I know my rights!"

The doctor pressed his lips together in irritation. "You do have rights, but we have also been granted the authority to detain anyone we believe to be a reasonable threat to public safety."

Bruce balked at this claim. "That's outrageous. Who approved that?"

"Governor Harris."

"Show me proof, and I'll cooperate. Otherwise, I'm going to make things difficult for you. I may be old," Bruce said, balling his hands into fists, "but I've got some fight in me yet."

The nurse pulled the doctor aside and whispered something to him. They conferred, and then the doctor nodded.

"Okay, Mr. Gentry. We'll be right back with a copy of the executive order, so that you can see that we truly have your best interest at heart."

Both of them left and closed the door, leaving Bruce alone with his wife. He dragged a chair to her bedside and sat down, clasping her hand in his. He flinched when he felt how cold and limp it was, as if she had already passed away. The monitors reflected a slow heartbeat, and Bruce studied the rise and fall of her chest to confirm she was still breathing.

The nurse returned with paperwork that seemed sufficient enough to Bruce, so he consented to being evaluated on the condition that he could remain in Helen's room. If he tested positive, he wouldn't be making her any sicker than she already was. If he tested negative, he'd wear protective gear. Either way, both he and the doctor knew that Helen was not long for this world, and what harm did it cause to let him remain by her side?

His test came back negative, so he donned the gear they gave him and took up residence beside her. Bruce only got up from his chair to use the bathroom and stretch his legs. Aside from that, he was sitting with her hand in his, waiting for what the hospice nurse said was soon to come.

Two days were spent like this.

On the third day, a commotion in the hallway drew Bruce's attention. He got up, needing to stretch his legs anyway, and saw that a patient had collapsed, knocking over a cart with food from the cafeteria. There was so much noise and confusion that he got distracted, and then saw what was on the TV in a neighboring room.

The local news was live, showing scenes from an on-going riot that was just a few blocks down from the hospital. A building was on fire, and a wall of Portland Police with riot shields raised were trying to push back an angry mob of distressed citizens.

Then, a thunderous explosion cut through the din of the overturned food cart, shaking the entire building around him. On the TV screen, the live feed had changed. It was like the camera had been dropped, the rakish angle showing a building that had been cratered by whatever had exploded, surrounded by a mass of people who had either been obliterated by the blast or severely injured.

The scene was painted in red, which Bruce knew to be blood.

He also knew that the chaos that was before the explosion was going to seem tame compared to the absolute pandemonium that was now going to begin.

Bruce ripped off his face shield and sterile paper gown and snagged a wheelchair from the hallway. He rushed back to Helen's bedside, determined to jailbreak her from this hospital, IV drip and all, so that he could keep her safe.

Except the monitor that reflected her heartbeat showed a single flat line. Other machines that monitored her vitals were making a chorus of beeps and chimes, alarms that were currently being ignored by the medical staff due to the chaos that now surrounded them.

Helen was dead, and she had died alone.

As he entered the room he saw that her eyes were open, and she had one hand stretched out toward the doorway where Bruce had been standing as he watched the TV's live report. The pain and guilt Bruce felt was enormous, and the weight of it crushed a part of him that would never recover.

With gentle hands he pulled her eyelids closed and tucked her arm back under her blanket. He shut off the monitors and machines, and draped a sheet over her.

Then, Bruce left. Alone.

That was the last time he had seen Helen, outside of in his memories and dreams, until now.

He knew it wasn't *his* Helen under that sheet, because he had left her behind at the hospital. Bruce tried to think about what might have happened to her body in the time since.

"I heard you, Helen," Bruce managed to say. "But I'm sorry, we can't go home."

Her head tilted to one side, dry muscle and bone creaking.

"Of course we can," she whispered, and held out her hand to him. "Let me show you."

It was the same hand she always offered him, when they would go for walks down back on their property, or when they would watch old movies together on their sofa. It was the same hand that reached out for him in the hospital when she was dying. She had wanted him then, by her side as he had been through 47 years of marriage, and the sight of her empty hand was too much for Bruce to bear.

He took her hand, which was little more than papery skin stretched over bone, and let Helen lead him toward the back of the foyer.

It was dark, far from the feeble light that came in through any nearby window. The only sound was that of his footsteps and the gentle *shushing* of the sheet dragging across the floor. Helen's feet made no sound at all, and Bruce wondered if she was floating.

"Here," Helen said after a moment, and stopped.

She released his hand, and then Bruce heard the sound of a doorknob turning.

The door swung open, releasing a burst of light so bright that Bruce clapped a hand over his eyes. Helen roughly pulled his hand down.

"Look," she said.

Bruce opened his eyes, squinting in the brilliant sunlight that streamed in through a set of wide windows. He recognized the room instantly.

It was their bedroom, from the home they had shared together their entire marriage. Bruce knew it was impossible, just like he knew the thing under the sheet standing next to him was not his wife. But he wanted so much for it to be that something ached deep within his chest.

Helen drifted inside and stood at the foot of the bed. Bruce followed, drawn in like iron filings to a magnet, barely registering that the door closed behind him.

Now inside, Bruce realized there was something wrong about this room. Everything seemed to be vibrating, as if the illusion of its very existence was struggling to maintain itself. It was disorienting, and Bruce felt the control he had over himself start to slip.

It felt like someone else was slipping their hand inside his mind, replacing him. Pushing him aside. The intruder was strong, and Bruce could not resist.

"Uncover me," she commanded.

The thought of seeing what was under the sheet struck Bruce with horror, but he watched from the sidelines within his mind as his body obliged her request.

The sheet fell to the floor. A hospital gown hung off her bony shoulders, which she untied and shrugged out of.

Helen stood before him, her emaciated figure just as he had suspected when he took her hand moments ago. She was a skeleton held together by yellowed skin. What remained of her hair, which she had kept long and straightened when she was alive, hung in

95

scraggly tangles. Some of it hung over her face, and he watched as she pulled it aside.

Bruce looked to where her eyes should have been, because that was the one way he thought he could know for sure if this was really her. Her eyes were nothing but empty sockets, dark voids that he felt would drive him to insanity if he looked at too long.

But this was already insane, wasn't it?

None of this was real. None of this was truly happening.

Bruce knew that, but he could do nothing about it.

Helen walked to her side of the bed and laid down.

"Join me," she said.

He did so without wanting to, fighting against whatever was in control of his body, but soon found himself laying down next to her.

"Do you remember what the pastor said on our wedding day?" she asked, cuddling in close to him. The sensation of her skin and bones against his body was horrid, and as he unwillingly pulled her in tight, his fingers pierced through the skin covering her ribcage.

Bruce screamed inside his mind, desperate to regain control, to push away the abomination that was masquerading as his wife, to leave this room, this house.

"He said now that we were married, we were one flesh. Do you remember that?"

Helen clacked her teeth together in a hideous grin.

"We are one flesh, Bruce, you and me," she whispered, "except I don't have flesh anymore."

Helen broke out of their embrace, pushing Bruce onto his back. She loomed over him, and Bruce felt something pierce his abdomen.

"You still do, however," Helen said.

The intruder in his mind made Bruce look down to see that she had jabbed a bony hand into the soft hollow of his stomach.

Helen plunged her other hand in and began to tear, and Bruce felt *everything*. His body rocked from side to side as she dug and ripped and pulled. His blood sprayed in great freshets across her, painting her a shade of red that had always been her favorite.

The blood-soaked skeleton of his dead wife, tearing him down to the bone, was the last thing Bruce saw. He felt something in his mind detach and realized it was his soul, and then there was, blissfully, nothing.

When her task was done, Helen laid down beside her husband, equals once again.

Part of Bruce remained, and he understood he was something like a ghost now. He was part of this damned house, doomed to be confined to it, to haunt it forever.

But he wasn't alone.

He had Helen by his side once more.

Bruce, not caring at all that the mattress was saturated with his blood, pulled Helen close to him, as he had done countless times in this bed they had shared when they had both been alive. He was pleased to discover that her skeletal embrace didn't repulse him at all this time.

In fact, it felt like home.

WESLEY

Wesley pushed the book off his lap and onto the mattress like it was a hot coal. He wanted nothing to do with it, and wanted more than anything to get away from the dead man who stood in front of him.

The man that he had stabbed to death, who was looking intently at him with unblinking, hollow eyes.

"I suppose you're wondering if I'm mad at you about…" the man paused, removed his hands from his abdomen, allowing his intestines and stomach to spill out, "well, all this. For the record, I'm not mad. I had pancreatic cancer, so I was on my way out anyway. You sort of did me a favor."

The man shuffled over to the bed, dragging his organs across the floor as he went, and sat next to Wesley. He nudged the book over so it rested between them, and Wesley's eyes rocked back and forth between the crimson tangle of intestines that hung out of the man's belly and the book that sat beside him.

"You really should read what happens next," the man said. "Unless you want it to be a surprise."

Wesley jumped up from the bed. "No, I can't! None of this makes any sense. This can't be happening."

"Ah, but it is," the man replied, picking up the book. He flipped to the back and put his finger on a page. "The next passage reads, *Wesley refused to read any further, too scared by what it might say. So, the man who had been Wesley's first murder victim began to read aloud.*"

Wesley shook his head. "No."

He turned his back to the man and caught his reflection in the mirror that was bolted to the wall over the sink. His ragged appearance gave him a start.

"*Wesley was shocked by his appearance in the mirror,*" the man read.

"Shut up, will you?" Wesley cried, whirling around. "I can't take this anymore!"

"*I can't take this anymore!*" the man read, in perfect unison and matching inflection with Wesley.

Furious, Wesley grabbed for the book and tore it out of the dead man's hands. The cover was sticky with blood. His flashlight still in hand, he looked at the page to see if what the man had been reading was truly in the book. Everything that had just happened was in there, just as he feared it would be.

Wesley took back the book and began to read it for himself. The dead man smiled at him from the bed and said to him, "I told you."

Wesley looked up at the man, who was displaying his teeth in a menacing grin. "I told you."

A pit formed in Wesley's stomach as he flicked his eyes back down to the open page.

Wesley heard a noise from behind him, a sound like someone knocking on a thick pane of glass.

As he read the words they came true, and Wesley turned toward the sound because that is what the book said he would do.

It was coming from the mirror, and Wesley wasn't the only one in its reflection anymore.

Standing behind him were all of the people he had killed. They were the ghosts that haunted his mind, and there were so many of them.

Wesley watched as one of them lifted a hand up to tap on his shoulder, and he screamed when he actually felt it *thump* upon his skin. He spun around, brandishing his flashlight like a dagger, and found that the gathering of his victims weren't just reflections.

They were in the room with him.

"Read," they said, their collective voices rumbling in the small room like thunder. "Read the words."

Wesley understood there was no point in arguing, so he did as he was told. The crowd of his victims closed in behind him as he read.

Throughout his life, Wesley had wondered from time to time about his death. When it would happen, what it would be like, and if there would be any pain. For someone who had inflicted much pain upon others, Wesley had little tolerance for it himself. He pondered this as he read, but with an urgent sense of fear in his heart. Still standing in front of the mirror, Wesley looked nervously at his reflection again and saw not himself, but the image of an old man with a neatly trimmed, thin mustache.

He looked vaguely familiar, but the knowledge of who he was escaped Wesley's grasp.

"Don't let the ghosts and the ghouls disturb you," the old man said.

Wesley was too startled to reply.

"It's almost time to lock up," the old man continued, "and then your party will really begin. I wonder how it will end."

Wesley blinked, and the reflection of the old man disappeared.

Confused, Wesley turned around, searching for meaning in the blank faces of his victims. He found nothing, and fear grew within him. He dropped the book and raced for the door, and just as he reached it, the sound of a bolt sliding closed in the door made him skid to a halt.

THE HOUSE THAT REMAINS

It was a sound Wesley had become familiar with during his various incarcerations.

When he was in prison, his cell was locked on a fixed schedule. He could count the minutes until it would be unlocked again, and the ritual of counting down until it was time for outdoor recreation or time for chow gave him some semblance of control. It was the same at Spring Meadow. They locked the residents in their rooms at night, or at least the dangerous ones like him, but he knew that they would be unlocked again when it was time for morning meds.

It all happened like clockwork, but here, in this house... Wesley had a sickening feeling that there was no one coming back to unlock it. He had a feeling that he was going to be trapped in this room for the rest of his life.

Wesley began to hyperventilate as icy panic took hold of him.

"You heard the man," one of his victims said, though half of his face was caved in from where Wesley had struck him with a baseball bat. "Let's get this party started."

Someone ripped the book out of his hands, and the group of Wesley's ghosts swarmed upon him, squeezing so close that Wesley couldn't move, could barely even breathe.

All of this happened inside Wesley's mind.

In reality, there was no painstakingly accurate recreation of his room at the mental hospital, there was only a barren wine cellar. There was no squad of his murder victims seeking posthumous revenge.

There was only Wesley, standing alone in the dark.

Screaming.

101

APRIL

The first thing April became aware of was that her head was pounding. Her pulse made her skull feel like it was swelling and releasing, but the very presence of that pain informed her of one important fact: she was alive.

Her unconsciousness had been dark and empty, a void that felt like dreamless sleep. It definitely hadn't been sleep, because every muscle in her body felt battered and exhausted. April slowly stretched and got up from the floor. She immediately checked her holster for her pistol and breathed a quick sigh of relief to find it still there.

The room she was in felt massive, her feet shuffling on the floor sending off echoes. There was no light, at least not by way of lamps or sconces, but everything was draped in a cloak of dark blue luminance. April allowed for her eyes to adjust to the environment and turned a slow circle to see who, or what, was in this place with her.

As far as she could see, she was alone.

It just didn't *feel* like she was.

April felt a pair of eyes on her, and it made her skin crawl. She wanted to find something to hide under or behind, but there was nothing nearby.

"Who's out there?" she cried, but only her echo responded.

She felt around in her pockets for her backup flashlight, nothing more than a keychain really, but it was better than nothing, especially in a place like this. The feeble light it offered didn't reveal much, but what it did show made April scream.

In front of her, arranged in a circle, were six stone platforms. A body rested on all but two of them, and once April recovered from her initial shock, she immediately knew what she was looking at.

The bodies were those of her group, and they were all dead.

April, despite knowing these five men for only a short period of time, felt anguish in her heart at knowing that her worst fears had come true.

She had been grateful to find a group of travelers that all seemed decent and trustworthy. As they circled around a small fire on their first night as a group of six, April listened to each of their stories. Brief as they were, it became apparent to her that they all shared something in common.

In the bleak, lawless world they found themselves in, all of them were afraid of being alone.

It was what made their kinship so strong, what made trusting this group of strangers so uncharacteristically easy for April to do. They bonded over this primal need for each other, and they had become a family despite no blood or legal union shared between them.

Looking at the platforms that bore the bodies of her friends, April never felt so utterly and desperately alone.

She knew, after what she had seen in that upstairs hallway, that the house was to blame. There was something about this house that was innately wrong, intrinsically evil.

This house had been a trap for them, not the safe haven they had wanted it to be.

"What is this place?" April asked aloud, not expecting an answer.

"This is the place where nightmares are born," came a reply, and from directly behind her.

She swung around and saw Dustin, his arms down at his side, his head slumped to one shoulder on his broken neck.

"And thanks to your comrades over there, we might live to see another day," he continued. "Well, *live* isn't really the right word, but I'm sure you catch my drift. Nothing really lives in here, not for long, anyway. That's how it works."

"How what works?"

"This house."

Dustin advanced a few steps closer, and April backed up in kind. He carried with him a smell that was oppressive and foul, like something that had been unburied that had no place being above ground.

"Its continued existence depends solely on those who make the mistake of walking in through those front doors. Considering how scarce resources were after the last place, we landed here more out of necessity than for anything else. We were weakened, and needed a place to rest. Recharge, if we're lucky. To be honest, if it hadn't been for you and your group of wanderers, we'd probably be dead."

"You sound like a crazy person," April said, taking a few more steps backward, aware that Dustin was pushing her closer to the stone platforms.

Dustin's face twisted with annoyance. "Don't believe me? Let me be clear, then. This house, this *manor*, we feed on the energy of the people we kill. We consume their fear, and are rejuvenated by the blood that gets spilled."

April tripped over an unseen object on the floor and fell, losing her backup flashlight in the process.

"That's why *I'm* here," Dustin said. "I'm here because I am what scares you most. That I'm not really dead, that someday I'm going to show up where you least expect it and finally take from you everything you refused me."

April shook her head, trying to get back to her feet, but she kept slipping. The ground was wet, and there were clods of dirt that made her hands slick.

"There's no sense in denying it. We know it's true." Dustin stopped advancing toward. "That's how we managed to clean house, if you pardon the pun, with the rest of your group. Once we found what scared them the most, the rest was easy."

"You keep saying 'we', but I only see you," April said. "You're not making any sense."

At this, Dustin laughed. His laughter boomed and rolled like thunder. It crashed and echoed off the distant walls, and then he suddenly stopped.

"Look again," he said, and a bolt of lightning split the sky above.

In the brief moment of illumination that the lightning offered, April saw that they were in a massive greenhouse. The walls on three sides were thick panes of glass, as was the roof above. Another strike showed her the rows and rows of raised garden beds that surrounded her, the soil within them dry and barren. A third strike gave more detail on the stone platforms that bore the bodies of her group, which encircled a large well, its mouth yawning wide and bottomless.

Bolts of lightning struck the ground repeatedly outside, some striking the iron that joined the panes of glass together. The strikes became nearly constant, strobing and filling the room with disorienting flashes. As April covered her eyes with her hands, she saw something reflected in the glass. She didn't want to accept what she was seeing, wanted to write it off as some trick of light and shadow.

Reflected in the glass was an army of ghosts. Hundreds, perhaps even thousands of them. April didn't need an explanation to know that these were the souls this house had claimed, and that they were all trapped here, forever.

"Like I said," Dustin gloated, his voice booming over the din. *"We."*

WESLEY

Wesley fought against the demons in his mind, pushing himself beyond the point of exhaustion as his adversaries were relentless. His brain had turned against him, an imaginative battle raging within the confines of his shattered psyche. In this delusion, several days elapsed in the span of only minutes. His mind told his body that he had gone without food, without sleep, without water, for nearly a week. His body, overpowered, reacted in kind.

One by one his internal organs began shutting down, and whatever fat and muscle he carried on his already slender frame started to wither away. In the interest of self-preservation, Wesley's body cannibalized itself to stay alive, even though what was happening felt like slow-motion suicide.

Wesley's mind had always been his most dangerous weapon. He used it to be cunning, to out-think and out-smart people, so that he could use them and take them down. The moment he first felt his blade pierce the skin of that man at the grocery store, he was no longer capable of compassion for his fellow man, or for any other human life.

People were no longer dentists or bus drivers or grocery store stock boys. They were either roadblocks or stepping stones. Wesley would either push his way through, or use you to get closer to what he wanted most, even if that meant spilling a little blood.

Especially if it meant spilling blood.

He never felt more alive than he did when he was doing his work. He had forgotten what it felt like, being weighed down by strong pharmaceuticals for so long. Everything felt muted and slow, and as he began rationing his medication, Wesley became addicted to it all over again.

Except now, his brain was overdosing.

Wesley could offer no defenses against this stronger part of himself. Every attempt he made at freeing himself from the throng of his attackers was futile, because they were just as much a part of him as he was. When his last bit of energy was expended, his muscles fully atrophied, his vision nearly gone from his body attacking even his optic nerves, Wesley collapsed to the floor.

His demons, those he had killed once upon a time, sensed his defeat and stopped their assault. They retreated into the dark corners of the room, which Wesley now saw was completely empty, and were gone.

Wesley cried out in anguish, knowing he was on the precipice of death, and he was terrified of what was to happen next. Death had always been something he had caused for others, and had been an abstract concept for him until now. This is what dying felt like, a steadily increasing vignette of absolute permanence.

He rolled onto his stomach and saw the book, *his* book, the book that would tell him how he was going to die. It was just outside of his grasp, and he dragged his shriveled body toward it.

Like before, the book was open to the last few pages.

He wasn't afraid of what the book might say anymore. In fact, he hoped he might find some solace in knowing what was to come next. There was only one thing on the horizon for him, and knowing exactly what was to come would be a small comfort. When it was finally within reach, he dragged it across the stone floor and under his face.

Wesley squinted to focus his eyes, barely able to discern the words on the page. His eyes roved slowly from left to right. As he read, he began to laugh.

It started low, barely more than a chuckle, and then grew. Great peals of it racked his bony shoulders as he propped himself up onto his elbows. Bones, weakened by his body's malnutrition, broke as his laughter rose in haunting crescendo. He choked on spit and coughed, his displaced mirth coming out in chortles and chuffs until he could barely breathe. By the time he had read through the last page, his maniacal laughter had driven him to tears.

"*That's* how I die?" he asked.

Wesley pushed the book aside, dragged himself across the room to his backpack, which had been all but forgotten, and pulled out a knife. Without any hesitation, he plunged it into his chest.

Piercing the heart would yield the fastest result, Wesley knew, and still allow him enough consciousness to feel it. Dehydrated, Wesley's blood was thick, syrupy. It pooled on his chest and then trickled down his sides.

As he bled out, Wesley smiled.

He smiled because knowing what was to happen, what the book foretold, eliminated all of the fear he felt about dying. It clarified a concept that had eluded him, and it was an ending that he actually looked forward to.

For him, death wasn't going to be the end. It was going to be transformation.

Wesley's heartbeat slowed, and then stopped. A ragged sigh pushed out of his lungs, the byproduct of his final breath, and he lay still.

Dead.

Nearby, a river of his blood was soaking through the pages of the book.

As Wesley died, the energy that remained within his cooling body was too strong to be contained any longer. Wesley rose out of himself, the withered flesh that had contained him, and saw that he was not alone. He was surrounded by the sprits of those who had been claimed by Price Manor, those souls trapped within the confines of this house of prey.

In life, he had grown accustomed to feeling isolated, that no one else was like him. Even as an in-patient at Spring Meadow, Wesley felt as if the burden of hiding his true self was nearly impossible to bear. But now…

Now, in death, Clive Wesley was among his kin.

Monsters and murderers, bringers of pain, shepherds of death, the legion of the dead who serve the will and demand of Price Manor, have a new soldier in their ranks.

Wesley felt an electric strength mix with the absolute and pervasive thirst that he knew could only be quenched with blood, freshly spilled. He knew that his death, here in Price Manor, was a destiny that suited him perfectly.

His instincts, now heightened, told Wesley that there was only one soul left in this house to take. He turned to his newfound company and asked: "Where is she?"

The pages in the book soaked up Wesley's blood eagerly, turning from cream to crimson, and one by one the legion of trapped souls in the room vanished.

They had been summoned to the greenhouse.

APRIL

Giving up was never an option April ever considered. There was nothing in her life that she had encountered thus far that was something she couldn't overcome, either by way of stubbornness or sheer determination. She had endured so much, had been tested to what she thought were her physical and emotional limits, but she continued to push herself even further because if she didn't fight back, didn't stand up for herself, no one else would.

She had always managed to make it through, to live to fight another day. Not always unscathed, of course. Some experiences left scars on her body, others within her mind, but she often reminded herself of an idiom her father used to say.

Every day above ground is a good one.

And now, trapped inside a house hell-bent on destroying every living soul within in it, surrounded by a veritable army of menacing souls and spirits, April didn't find as much comfort in the idiom as she had in the past.

She had once thought surviving Dustin was going to be the worst thing in her life she had to endure. She had prayed for that to be the case, in fact, because the constant fear she lived in was a burden unlike any other.

Every noise in her house at night was him, having broken into her apartment somehow. Every unknown caller on her phone was him, as changing his cell number was a tactic he frequently used to try to contact her. Every car that drove too close behind her in traffic was him. Every guy with a similar build and hair color was him. Her employer, whom she informed about his behavior and the subsequent restraining order, did nothing beyond moving Dustin to another department. She became afraid that she'd bump into him in the breakroom, or in the hallway, or in the parking lot.

It remained this way until civilization collapsed, until she put an entire magazine worth of bullets into his chest when he did finally break in. April had felt that there would never be any escape from him, but she never gave up. The moment she was finally free from him, and free because she hadn't backed down despite the crippling fear she felt, was one she'd never forget.

But all of this now, being trapped in a situation she thought would have only been possible in one of John's horror novels, just might take the cake.

The lightning and thunder faded, but an eerie green hue remained. The undead stood in rank and file behind Dustin, as if he were their commander.

If he is their leader, April thought, stifling a smirk, *then I might have a fighting chance of getting out of this alive. They don't know what a blazing idiot he is.*

"As you can see, we've got you outnumbered," Dustin said. "And if you look behind you, it seems that one more of your friends has joined us."

She turned and saw that one of the two empty stone platforms now bore a body.

That meant she was the last one.

April had never put much effort into hoping that someone was going to come to her aid, because even though she had always been surrounded by people who could help, no one ever did. Now, in a rapidly escalating situation where there was literally no one else on her side,

April was surprised at how much that shook her. It was, once again, up to her to fight for survival.

She kept her eyes fixed on the stone platforms, her mind furiously thinking of how to escape.

"Hey, you newcomers," Wesley cried out. "Why don't you come join us?"

April turned to Dustin, wondering who he was speaking to, and when she turned back to the platforms, she saw that the bodies that rested upon them began to move.

And they weren't really bodies so much anymore.

They were remains.

John rose first. His massive frame was covered in lesions, wide and torn open sores that revealed valleys of rot and decay. He opened his mouth, and April saw his tongue was gone, having been eaten through by a pool of festering pus, which leaked past his split lips and down his chin. His legs were broken at the shins and crumpled underneath his bulk in opposing directions.

Brady was next, and he was covered in dirt. Worms and grubs wriggled out from every part of his body. They tumbled out of his ears and nostrils, some squeezing their way out of his tear ducts. His mouth was full of spiders, which spread out like a many-legged blanket over him.

To Brady's side was a skeleton. Scraps of muscle and ligament still clung to various bones, but it was the slightly hunched posture of them that told April that this was Bruce.

Tim pushed off his platform in a great rush of water. It poured from him, his skin bloated and full from the water that had drowned him. There were a series of deep wounds on his chest, and from those wounds came red leaves.

And last, there was Wesley. He reminded April of Gollum, so shrunken and deformed. Whatever had caused his death was surely a painful one, but the smile on his face told April that he had, somehow, enjoyed it.

They all remained in front of their platforms, as if they were waiting for permission to move closer. A crack of thunder broke directly overhead, making April flinch, and a bolt of lightning immediately followed. She squeezed her eyes shut in the sudden brightness, and when she reopened them, the five dead men had jumped forward. They were nearly within arm's reach, and Wesley took an uneven step forward.

"I was promised a meal," he hissed, "and I'll be damned if you don't look *delicious*."

April backpedaled and immediately bounced off Dustin. He had closed the gap while she was distracted, and she screamed when his head ricocheted forward and his face pressed against her neck. She felt his tongue flick against her skin and threw her shoulder back, trying to push him away, but he had wrapped his arms around her waist.

"Hold her still so I can get a taste," Wesley said, creeping closer. His arms, muscles shrunken and fixed tight in a praying position, lunged toward her. His fingernails were long and bitten down to jagged points.

Dustin tightened his grip, but April managed to get her right arm free just before. She reached back for her pistol and drew it from the holster. She raised it up and was wrapping her finger around the trigger when Wesley swatted it out of her hand. Her finger, just barely hooked around the trigger, squeezed back and the gun fired.

The sound of gunfire reverberated across the room. April felt Dustin's grip loosen just a little and saw her opportunity. She threw her arms outward and turned her shoulder as hard as she could, using her momentum to throw Dustin off her back and into Wesley. They struck each other with a satisfying *thud* and fell to the floor.

April looked wildly around for her pistol and saw it on the floor, just a few feet away from where Dustin and Wesley lay tangled together. She thought about trying to grab it, but didn't want to risk getting too close. It hurt her to leave it behind, but she knew it was the right choice. If she was to ensure her survival now, she'd have to rely on something else.

She sprinted away, toward the wall that joined the greenhouse with the rest of the manor. The sea of ghosts that had gathered stood between her and the door, but she could see no other way out other than to go through them. She tucked her chin and pushed herself to run faster.

A roar of determination and fear ripped out of her throat as she ran.

April thought of all the nights she had spent alone and afraid, clutching her pistol in one hand under her pillow just in case Dustin showed up. She thought of all the times she chose a seat in the back of the room so she could see the door. She thought of the way no one took her seriously when she enrolled in her handgun course. She thought of how no one ever had her back, and how no one had ever fought for her.

She thought these things, and she smiled.

It was because of these things that she had the strength and the courage to do what she had to do in this moment. The last few years of her life, all of the struggles and sleepless nights, the anxiety and paranoia, all of it had been in preparation for *this*.

The fight for her life.

April dove headfirst into the crowd of ghosts, expecting to have to fight each of them off, but she ran through them like a thick fog. They tried to stop her, as she could feel hands pulling on her clothes, her backpack, and her hair, anything that they could reach. It slowed her down but she didn't stop.

"Stop her!" Wesley cried from behind.

"Grab her now!" Dustin added.

April risked a glance over her shoulder and saw that they had gotten up from the floor and were giving chase.

She also saw that the raised garden beds, which were spread out across the room in every direction, were shaking. A hand burst out from under the dirt in one of them, and then another. Soon, all across the room, hundreds of rotting corpses in various stages of decay climbed out from under the dry dirt.

At once, the spirit-fog evaporated as the ghosts rejoined the bodies they had left behind.

April realized then that this wasn't a greenhouse after all.

This was a graveyard.

She whipped her head back around, pumping her legs even harder. Her lungs burned, but the door was just a few strides away. She reached it seconds later, slamming into it at full speed. April bounced off and fell.

The stone floor trembled under the footsteps of the approaching army of the dead, Dustin and Wesley leading the charge.

April sprang to her feet, wincing at the sudden pain in her ankle. She forced herself to ignore it, focusing instead on trying to work the doorknob with her shaking hands. At last the knob turned and she pulled the door open.

She found herself in another hallway, and it was on fire. Flames rippled up the walls in every direction, crawling across the ceiling in a complete inferno. April stopped just outside the door, the intense and oppressive heat in the hallway like an invisible wall.

The only way forward was wreathed in fire. Her only real option was to go back into the graveyard, toward the throng of angry corpses, which she knew would mean certain death. And surely a gruesome one, at that.

"Fuck that," April said. She slammed the door, leaving the graveyard behind, and ran headlong into the fire. Crouching below the rolling flames, she was unsure of what lay ahead but hoped it was better than what was behind her.

As she ran, doors to her left and right opened wide. Instead of being full of the horrible things she had witnessed earlier, the rooms appeared to be empty. She knew better than to trust them to be safe, because she now understood that nowhere in this house was.

Ahead, a blast of flames tore through a wall. Plaster, splintered wood, and other debris flew through the air toward April. She ducked but couldn't avoid all of it, grunting and crying out in pain as she was struck by a shard of wood that plunged deep into her shoulder.

The explosion left behind a jagged hole in the wall directly ahead, where the hallway continued to the right, and through it she saw the most beautiful thing she had ever seen in her life.

A hayfield.

Lit up by the rising morning sun, April couldn't believe it. This was her way out of this place, her means of escape.

Then, as she planted her foot to jump out into the field, her injured ankle shattered and she collapsed. She cried out in pain, bellowing as the wooden shard in her shoulder buried itself deeper when she hit the floor.

"There she is!" she heard someone yell, and saw that her pursuers had caught up to her. They were unfazed by the fire, walking through it like it wasn't there at all.

April wasn't so lucky.

She felt the flames on her skin, felt her skin start to bubble and blister. The pain in her ruined ankle was forgotten in the face of this new, searing agony, but what she saw coming down the hall toward her was worse still.

Dustin and Wesley pushed to the front of the crowd. Dustin's head slumped to one side, the stump of his broken spike now piercing through the skin of his neck. Wesley hobbled along next to him, licking his lips, and pushed ahead.

"Don't forget, she's mine!" Wesley said and then breathed in through his nose. "Can you smell that? She's cooking!"

The pain April felt as she burned was overwhelming. She tried crawling toward the hole in the wall, but her clothing had fused to her skin and then melted to the carpeted floor.

Like a fly caught in a spider's web, April was trapped.

She closed her eyes.

Long ago, April vowed that she would never give up. Quitting was never an option she gave herself in her mind, because there always was a way to persevere.

Her mind spun with how quickly things had changed, and with the understanding that this, and here in this house, was the end.

April told herself that she wasn't giving up; she was giving in.

A thunderous roar drowned out the sound of the inferno.

April opened her eyes and looked up to see a great flood of water surging down the hallway, extinguishing the fire. The hallway filled with smoke and steam, and in the gray cloud that billowed toward her, she saw Tim.

He rode on the crest of a wave like Poseidon, and sent a monstrous wave directly toward her. April had time enough to pull in a deep breath before the water crashed over her. It was frigid in contrast to the furnace that almost claimed her life, and it snuffed out the fire that had been spreading over her.

The water receded and April sputtered to the surface. Remnants of the wave that saved her spilled out of the hole in the wall like a waterfall, but April noticed that the hole was getting smaller. The house was repairing itself, not only closing off April's option for escape, but causing the water level in the hallway, water that came from an unknown source, to rise.

With her injuries, April could do little more than float. She craned her neck and saw that Dustin and Wesley, along with the rest of their army, were still trying to get to her. The water slowed them down, but still they approached. The current of the water led all of them down the hallway until there was no hallway left.

With nowhere else to go, the rising river pooled in the dead end and rose even higher, pushing April closer and closer toward the ceiling.

"April."

She recognized Tim's voice, and tried to find where it was coming from. She bumped into the wall and spun around, and then saw him.

Tim was standing in front of a curtain of water, his arms spread wide. He appeared to be holding everyone back, but April could also see that he was, inexplicably, controlling the water. Although bruised and bloated, April noted the exhaustion and determination that creased his face.

Was he, like everyone else he was holding back, wanting to claim her for himself?

"What are you doing?" she yelled.

"Runoff River," he said, more water spilling out of his mouth. The wounds on his chest and torso split open into wide gashes, polluting the water with red leaves. The current brought them toward her, turning the blueish water crimson.

April dipped under the surface for a moment, coughing her lungs clear when she resurfaced.

"What does that mean?" she cried.

Tim grimaced, and then sent more water toward her.

"Rrrunoff... riv..." he said, struggling to speak under the effort.

"Tim, I don't understand!"

His arms lowered for just a moment, but that was enough for Dustin to push his way through. His head drooped down into the water as he paddled closer, parting the leaves that flowed out of Tim's body.

Tim bellowed and raised his arms back up, and in doing so he lifted a ridge of water up in front of Dustin, pushing him back and away from April, who looked on in disbelief.

From across the ocean that separated them, April and Tim locked eyes.

"Rrr... *Run*," he said.

Something deep underneath April groaned, and then the house shuddered. Before she had time to realize what was happening, she was caught in the downdraft of a vortex.

The floor underneath her had broken under the immense weight of the water, which was now rapidly draining. As she spun, drifting closer to the center and rapidly building speed, she saw Tim holding Dustin and Wesley and all of the other exhumed soldiers back. They were attacking him, tearing him apart.

Tim had fought for her, when no one else had.

And then she was falling, falling.

Falling.

As before, there were things April became aware of when she regained consciousness.

First, everything *hurt*.

Second, and most importantly, she felt a warm, gentle breeze caressing her cheek.

So I'm alive, she thought.

April opened her eyes and slowly recognized where she was: on the floor in the foyer of Price Manor. She was soaked, and was lying in a puddle peppered with red leaves. Her heart skipped when she saw that the heavy double doors had been pushed wide open from the deluge that came from upstairs, that had carried her with it.

Through the doorway she saw again the hayfield, the tall grass undulating in the breeze that traced its way up the walkway.

It looked like heaven.

April was grateful to be alive, grateful even for the pain. Her brain felt jumbled, but the image of Tim sacrificing his soul to allow her this opportunity to escape was still very clear. In fact, his sacrifice was something she thought she would never forget.

As tired as she was, and despite the excruciating pain she felt across every part of her body, she knew she could not remain where she was. There were still forces in this house that wanted her dead, and given that she had no idea how long she was unconscious for, the manor's militia could be just upon her.

Run, Tim had said.

April didn't think she could run, but she made herself get to her feet nonetheless, because she knew this was her final chance. She shuffled to the doorway, crying out in pain with every step that jostled her broken ankle, and felt the floor under her vibrate, as if the house knew she was getting away.

The hayfield outside began to shimmer. April attributed it to the vibration playing tricks with her eyes, but then she saw something else outside. The hayfield was gone, replaced for just an instant by a sprawling lawn and vibrant gardens, and then the hayfield snapped back. The two scenes switched back and forth rapidly as April reached the doorway. She was breathless, desperate for the freedom that was almost within her grasp. One of them she knew, the bleak dystopian world that was nearly as dangerous as the house she was trying to escape. The other was completely unknown.

April jumped over the threshold, broken ankle and burns be damned, not caring which freedom she got.

PRICE MANOR: EPILOGUE

If its appearance caused a shockwave, the disappearance of Price Manor caused a vacuum. In the field, which had once been referred to as belonging to God, nothing (and no one) remained.

ELIZABETH

The air conditioner in the window sputtered, trying valiantly to keep up with the August heat but falling short. An oscillating fan perched on a nearby desk circulated the tepid air, and Elizabeth brushed her sweaty bangs off her forehead. She sat facing the door, waiting for it to open.

Shannon, who was standing in front of the AC, sighed dramatically.

"How much longer, do you think?" she asked.

Elizabeth, who had been distracted by her intent focus on the door, pried her eyes from it and looked at Shannon.

"What did you say?"

"I asked you how much longer this heat was going to last. I'm melting over here."

Elizabeth shrugged and returned her attention back to the door. "I don't know. Google it."

"What the hell does that mean?"

A brief trill of anxiety struck Elizabeth, but she pushed it down. "Sorry. Got my words messed up. I meant check the forecast, it's probably in there." She gestured to a folded newspaper resting on the corner of the desk.

Shannon sat down in the chair next to Elizabeth and grabbed the newspaper, opting to fan herself with it instead.

"I swear, you say the weirdest things sometimes.," she said.

"I know," Elizabeth said. "I'm sorry, I'm just distracted. Nervous."

"Excited, too, I hope?"

Elizabeth looked at her friend, who was also her lawyer.

"Yes, I'm very excited," Elizabeth said, and smiled.

They had met in the hospital a few months prior. Shannon had been summoned to speak with a woman who, after waking from a week-long coma, was unsure of not only where she was, but *when* she was and *who* she was. She was patient and kind with Elizabeth, and helped her sort things out.

As to *where* she was, she was in Maine General Medical Center in Augusta.

As to *when* she was, it was the year 1995.

As to *who* she was...

She was brought in as a Jane Doe by a Good Samaritan (who she'd later find out was the Postmaster for Webster's Mills). Barely alive, with bruises and scrapes and burns over most of her body, she had no identification on her person. But if you looked past her injuries, she fit the description of a missing person named Elizabeth Walker.

According to Shannon, Elizabeth Walker was unmarried and lived alone, and had been reported missing by her employer two weeks prior. Local authorities had been trying to locate her, as she was the only next of kin to a boy who, following a recent and brutal murder-suicide, had been made an orphan. Her reappearance saved the boy from entering the foster system.

It was a convenient solution to a very unique problem.

And now, she was waiting anxiously for a boy who would soon be her sole responsibility. She had never pictured herself as a mother, but she was not one to give up in the face of a challenge. She had survived far worse, surely she could survive this.

The door to the small office they were waiting in opened and swung wide.

Irene, their social worker, stood in the doorway, holding the hand of a small boy. She crouched next to him and gave him a big smile.

"Timothy, I'd like for you to meet your Aunt Elizabeth, and her lawyer, Shannon Hayes."

There was fear and distrust on the boy's face that Elizabeth recognized, for it was one she had seen on her own face many times. Elizabeth smiled and offered her hand. The boy looked down at her hand and then retreated behind Irene.

Her skin, while healed, still reflected the burns she had suffered. That part of her life, her exodus from that horrible place, felt like it happened ages ago, but it haunted her still. Normally she wore long sleeves to cover them up, but the recent heat wave demanded short sleeves.

"I'm sorry," Irene said, "but as I've shared, he's been through a lot. It might take him a few minutes to warm up to you." She led Timothy into the room, directed him to a nearby sofa, and then closed the door.

Shannon and Irene spoke, words that were only sounds to Elizabeth. She was focused on the boy, whose tragic story was replaying in her mind. Elizabeth rose from her chair and pointed to an open spot on the sofa.

"Can I sit with you?" she asked Timothy.

He looked at Irene, who nodded, and then back to Elizabeth.

"Yes," he said.

Elizabeth sat, allowing for as much space between them as she could so as to not crowd him. Shannon and Irene continued their conversation, covering all of the details and logistics that Elizabeth couldn't care less about. None of that mattered, not as much as this little boy did.

"I heard what happened," she said, keeping her voice low. "I'm so sorry you had to go through that."

Timothy looked at her, his wide eyes cautious.

"But surviving bad things, that's something you and I have in common," Elizabeth continued, and gestured to the scars and burns that trailed up her arms, disappearing under her clothes, and then reappearing on her legs. "We both know what it's like to go through things that are really scary, and you know what? We're both still here."

That seemed to loosen something up within the boy, and his shoulders relaxed. He still stared at her scars, but that was okay. He had scars of his own, and though they were not visible like hers, Elizabeth could still see them.

"You know what else?" she asked.

"What?"

"I used to know a man named Tim once."

"You did?"

Elizabeth nodded. "He was funny, loved to tell jokes."

The boy gave her a timid smile.

"He was also very brave," Elizabeth said, "And I have a feeling you are pretty brave, too."

Tears welled up in the boy's eyes, and this time when Elizabeth held out her hand, he took it eagerly. His hand trembled in hers, which was just as well. It matched the trembling she felt in her heart.

The conversation between Shannon and Irene lapsed, and Elizabeth looked up at them. Irene seemed pleasantly surprised.

"I can see that we're off to a good start," she said.

"It sure seems that way. What do you think, Elizabeth?" Shannon asked.

Elizabeth and Tim shared a look, and then a smile.

"I think he's perfect."

There was some paperwork to sign. Elizabeth signed first, and then Shannon as witness.

Elizabeth Walker, she wrote, which still felt foreign to her, but she was getting used to it.

And with that, Irene rose from her chair behind the desk.

"You ready, Timothy?" she asked.

He got up from the couch and took Elizabeth's hand in his.

"I'm ready," he said. "Let's go home."

Elizabeth, who (in another time, in another world) had been called April, took this boy into her heart, preserving the life of the man she knew he would become: a man who (in another time, in another world) had once saved her life.

THE END

June 16th, 2022 – August 4th, 2022

MICHAEL R. GOODWIN

PRICE MANOR WILL CONTINUE...

THE HOUSE THAT REMAINS

Coming Soon:

THE HOUSE THAT REMEMBERS

THE NEXT BOOK IN THE PRICE MANOR SERIES

from KELLY BROCKLEHURST

ABOUT THE AUTHOR

Michael R. Goodwin is the author of several books, such as THE LIBERTY KEY and SMOLDER, and two short story collections, HOW GOOD IT FEELS TO BURN and ROADSIDE FORGOTTEN. He lives in Maine with his wife, their four children, and more animals than he can count.

Find out more information about him and his books on his website: michaelrgoodwin.com

Follow him on Instagram @michaelrgoodwin, where he tries his hardest to not be socially awkward.

Made in the USA
Middletown, DE
07 April 2023

28083419R00076